Meeting Coty

RUTH ESTEVEZ

What's your favourite perfume?

Ruth Estevez x

Beaten Track
www.beatentrackpublishing.com

Meeting Coty

Second Edition
Published 2022 by Beaten Track Publishing
First edition published 2007
Copyright © 2007, 2022 Ruth Estevez

Paperback ISBN: 978 1 78645 532 1
eBook ISBN: 978 1 78645 533 8

Cover Design: Debbie McGowan (adapted from 'Les Eaux de Cologne parfumées de Coty', copyright © 1950 Fernando Bosc).

Beaten Track Publishing,
Burscough, Lancashire.
www.beatentrackpublishing.com

Acknowledgements

There would be no *Meeting Coty* if my dad hadn't researched the Estevez family tree. As immigrants from Spain to the UK, family ties were broken due to place and circumstance, so to find out names and patchy details about the sherry importing business from the Estevez Bodega in Jerez de la Frontera, and learning names and snippets about family dynamics, meant my imagination caught hold. Thank you, Dad.

His research was pre-internet, so thank you to the Latter-day Saints Genealogy Library – Family History Records, which Mum and Dad viewed in Huddersfield, UK.

My great aunt Tessa did in fact work for the François Coty Corporation.

Thanks to Mum, for her undying faith in my writing and saying she'd never read anything like *Meeting Coty*.

Thanks to Louise at Coty UK for going beyond the call of duty with her help in researching François Coty.

Inspiration also comes from J. M. Barrie's characters of Peter and Wendy. Quotations in *Meeting Coty* are from Daniel O'Connor's *The Story of Peter Pan* – O'Connor's 1914 retelling of Barrie's fairy play. Thanks also to Barrie's play *Dear Brutus*, which is quoted here. While I was working in stage management at Pitlochry Festival Theatre, *Dear Brutus* was in the repertoire, and its theme of 'what might have been' has stayed with me.

First published in 2007, *Meeting Coty* fell out of print after my publisher at Kings Hart Books passed away. It was a friend in Ireland, a friend made over Facebook and never met, who encouraged me to bring the novella into the world again. Many thanks for giving me the confidence, and friendship, Carol Doherty.

Thanks to Jor Barrie for proofreading the final manuscript and spotting 'gilder' rather than 'glider' on the first line!

And finally, to Debbie McGowan, of Beaten Track Publishing for liking *Meeting Coty* enough to re-edit the story, update the cover design and republish it. Debbie makes it all look so easy. Thank you.

Meeting Coty

Chapter One

S USPENDED LIKE A small glider on a windless day, Tessa floated through the silent dining room, across the hallway, into the sunlit drawing room and back again. As her white-clad form passed by, she snapped blooms from the vast displays. She didn't hesitate once as she dropped each perfume-laden flower into the cotton basin that she'd made by pinching up the hem of her nightgown with her eight-year-old fingertips. She gathered her harvest with hardly a rustle, her undersized bare feet soundless on both carpet and wood and her figure glinting in the dark, polished surfaces and brass inlay handles of the sideboards.

Pausing at the foot of the stairway, she glanced with dark, hopeful eyes at the imposing front door. It was too early for the rattle of the milk cart. Too early for the postman. Too early to be downstairs alone in the Garcia household. But not too early to garrotte heady blooms from her mother's carefully arranged Covent Garden flowers.

She blossomed in the silence of the house and had made her flower harvesting at this hour a weekly ritual. She anticipated it, planned it, washed out the bottles begged from the cook, rearranged her sleep and waited patiently for dawn to rise the day after their delivery.

Less than twenty-four hours previously, she had dangled out of the nursery window as the Covent Garden van arrived, inadvertently angering her elder sister, Mariquita, with her apparent recklessness. Oblivious, Tessa hurried downstairs to the kitchen, where she hovered as Abigail, the family maid, lifted the lids off the long boxes. Peering inside, Tessa inhaled, while the cook paused, oven gloves mid-air, offended that someone could prefer the scent of flowers to her freshly baked cakes. Whilst little Carmen demanded to lick out the bowl, the middle Garcia daughter stored any dropped flower heads to carry away for further dissection.

Now, inwardly holding the peace of the house like the cradled blooms in the curve of her nightgown, Tessa turned from the front doorway and mounted the stairs. The second tread from the top creaked underfoot, and she paused, listening to hear if the air in the bedrooms stirred. It did not. Not this morning. Not this perfume-filled day.

Black-haired Mariquita snored, and auburn-headed Carmen lay abandoned to her dreams, the bedroom cocooned with warmth and sleep. Tessa's feet stepped exposed across the wood, then hidden over the rug and once more touched polished floorboards.

In the small bathroom that Mr. Garcia had insisted on installing for his daughters, she lowered the plug over the hole and turned the taps. Water washed into the day all the anticipated noise of the house. It bounced off the hard, white surfaces until it formed a pool that grew until it was a deep lake into which a tumble of scents cascaded. Blues and mauves, purples and cream, pinks and whites

2

and reds ranging from velvet to vermilion. Tessa sank her long fingers into the flower-filled depths. The petals stroked her hands under the water, and flower heads jostled against her wrists. She bowed over until her nose broke the surface, the rosy light reflected in her cheeks as she inhaled. In that inward breath, she sensed the fields where flowers grew in unleashed sweeps of scent. She flew with the bees, entering opaque boudoirs to douse herself in pollen and emerge saturated in honey-thick powder. Tilting her face to the warm sunshine, she wriggled her fingers in flight as colours began to merge.

"What are you doing?" Mariquita asked, her figure shadowed in the doorway.

Tessa turned, her arms prisoners to the flower wardens. She smiled as wide as a sunflower.

"Buenos dias, Mariquita."

Chapter Two

FORTY-FIVE-YEAR-OLD JOSEPH GARCIA popped a Liquorice Allsort into his mouth. He let the smooth, black cylinder roll around intact. He preferred the tangy black to the sweet, white filling. In some unconscious place, it reminded his senses of home. Of silent siestas where young boys could not sleep. Of darkened rooms and the sound of grasshoppers. The liquorice tasted warm and syrupy on his tongue like a long Jerez de la Frontera afternoon. He sat at his well-used desk in his study and savoured the start of the day.

ANNIE GARCIA LAY in bed with her eyes open. Her door, like her husband's, remained closed. However, even closed doors could not prevent the noise of the house from entering each room. Mrs. Garcia pulled the sheet and eiderdown and crocheted quilt up to her cheekbones and watched a beam of sunlight pierce through a gap in the curtains. Dusty particles randomly avoided each other in the light before the beam settled on the dressing table. A glass dragonfly shimmered.

WITH HER HANDS pressed over her ears, Tessa sat on the bottom stair in the hallway, facing the front door. From her point of view near the ground, the door was a vast barricade of impenetrable wood. It was not improved by a large cage suspended halfway down into which arrived, courtesy of a horizontal rectangle, the news from the outside world.

She was now dressed, and she knew, from the sounds of the house, that the other occupants were in various states of attire. She closed her eyes. Even with her hands over her ears and her eyes closed, she could still hear and see her brothers and sisters. Doors opened and closed; drawers were rifled through then rammed shut. Wardrobe doors and chairs and brushes and combs banged and rattled, all noisily used by eight pairs of hands—nine, including her own, but hers were still while she listened to all that noise. Without it, she felt scared. Hearing it, she wanted to scream. Too many sisters and brothers. And a mother, still as a sarcophagus in bed.

Their mother was a presence in the house that, despite its stillness, continually threatened to pounce. The assault was never anything but verbal, but it was stroked with acid. All the children waited. It was the only influence that silenced the noise. When it came, that torrent of ice over stones, it always thundered in the same direction, no matter what anyone else had done. It didn't matter that Tessa had ruined the flower displays; it must surely be Mariquita's fault. The others always hesitated, wondering if it might, on that particular occasion, be directed at one of them. They hoped, in spite of themselves, but apart from the odd stray shard, it never was.

Mrs. Garcia's torrent of anger was always aimed at the eldest daughter, Mariquita. Mariquita, who was more of a mother than Ann Loughlin, as their mother had previously been known, had ever been. The Garcia children did not hate her. They had built a dam to protect themselves from that, and they all knew she was rising behind that carefully constructed wall in which, despite their efforts, cracks were beginning to show. Mariquita did her utmost to repair the damage whenever the others weakened. The wall was now so patched it resembled the quilt on Mariquita's bed and because she stood closest to the barrier, the spray over the top caught her alone. On the day that the dam would eventually explode, the noise would be deafening, but they knew that more cracks would appear before then.

Tessa's eyes snapped open, and she bounded across the tiles towards the door. Stretching on her tiptoes, she released the latch, and although she heard someone from upstairs calling her name, she heaved open the front door. The postman smiled down at her.

"Good morning, Mr. Brookes."

"Good morning, Miss Teresa." He glanced over her head into the house. "I hear the Garcia family are in good voice, as usual."

She turned to follow the direction taken by his eyes.

Upstairs, in the boys' bedroom, Tony and Nacho were jumping off the bed onto the polished floor. By the window, a book slid accidentally from Frank's fingers as he reached to replace it on the shelf. Joseph slammed himself inside the bathroom. Matty dropped his boots, and laughing, Alfonso fell over them.

In the girls' bathroom, taps gushed water into the sink as Mariquita wiped away the remains of pollen, muttering under her breath.

"It's always me. Always me."

On the landing, at the top of the stairs, a doll hung precariously over the banister. Carmen opened her mouth. As she screamed, she let go of the doll, and it plummeted, landed on the tiles with a crack and lay broken next to its ragged friend.

Through all of this, Mrs. Garcia did not move from her bed. In the study, Mr. Garcia popped another Liquorice Allsort into his mouth.

Tessa held out her hands. "Papa is waiting."

Mr. Brookes presented her with the day's post and turned to walk back down the steps. Running down the hallway, Tessa flung open the study door and rushed inside.

"What have we today?" Mr. Garcia asked, closing the top drawer of his desk and smiling at the only daughter who appeared to take an interest in him.

She shuffled onto his knee and reached across the leather expanse for the letter opener. He waited patiently as she lifted each envelope carefully, sliced it open with the silver knife and placed each open missive onto a new pile. She again heard her name being called, but she ignored it, even though Mr. Garcia must have heard it too. When every envelope lay open, he looked at Tessa. She looked back at him. Although neither of them commented, they both knew what it meant, and after a moment, she jumped down and walked towards the door.

"Tessa!" her father called. She turned back to him. "Don't you want payment for a job well done?"

A black-and-white square spiralled through the air. She put her head back and, with mouth and eyes wide, caught it in her teeth. She turned, left cheek bulging with syrup and sugar, and re-entered the noise of the house.

Chapter Three

THE GARCIA GIRLS retreated to the nursery whenever they sought a vestige of quiet. It was a pale room with a solid door and lace curtains that obscured the outside world. The shelves held their well-thumbed books, boxes of paints and utensils with which to draw. Carmen's badly repaired dolls lay in a cot, caught in suspended sedation. Games frequently lay strewn across the floor in un-associated pieces until Mariquita tidied them away.

Rain battered the windows. Carmen knelt up on the window seat, reaching across the table to swish her paintbrush in a jar of brownish-purple water and then twirled it in the coloured palette before daubing an unidentifiable display on a rectangle of paper. Tessa had cut tiny squares and drawn on them delicate violets and roses. One had already been glued onto a bottle of insipid-coloured liquid, which had gathered a sediment of what looked like lavender grains, crushed rose petals and tiny spots of deep purple, all shrouded with a dusting of mould. Other similar bottles stood awaiting their labels and the flourish of a floral name to capture their scent. Tessa painted the drawings meticulously, carefully dipping the tip of her brush into an appropriate colour, with a little water to dilute it, and touching the paper in the chosen place. With a black ink pen, she wrote the perfumes' names: *La Rose Jackintot. Eau de Tessa. Corsica Flora.*

Mariquita sat on a stool at the other side of the room. Her eyes scanned the elaborate scrawl on the two sheets of paper in her hands. She held them side by side so that the *Dearest Mariquita* and *Your loving Grandmamma* were always in sight. She read silently, disregarding Carmen's discordant rhymes and Tessa's resounding concentration. Finally, when she had read every word, she cleared her throat and read the letter again, but this time aloud for her sisters to hear.

"*Dearest Mariquita, Teresa and Carmen...*"

"Why doesn't she say 'Tessa'?" asked Carmen.

"Because Tessa's proper name is Teresa," Mariquita said. "Shall I continue?" Carmen nodded and returned to her painting. Tessa didn't look up. "*Dearest Mariquita, Teresa and Carmen—*"

"You've read that bit."

Mariquita paused for barely a breath before continuing, but in that instant, instead of Carmen's questions, their relatives in Spain slipped into the room.

"*What a time we have had. You will be pleased to hear that your cousin Rosa is now married. It is perfect timing. The grapes are in and it is a good harvest. We all breathe easy because it doesn't matter whether it rains now or not. Of course, the sun shone for the wedding, and we prayed you all could have been with us, but I suppose your papa explained why that was not possible.*"

"Why was it not possible?" Carmen wanted to know.

"Business," said Tessa, adding yellow to a forget-me-not. "Papa is very busy with business."

"*Rosa looked very beautiful. The Perez family are lucky to have gained such a daughter-in-law. The babies will be ravishing if they take after her, as long as they do not have the misfortune to inherit the Perez chin. But they are not without money, so we can live with that. They, on the other hand, will have to live with Rosa's temper. I told her mother, she may be beautiful, but what is her temper for? She does not need it. Men take one look and give her what she wants. Old women, reminded of their own youthful good looks, find themselves doing her work, and children adore her because she is like a princess. We all adore her, but she insists on throwing her temper across the table for all to hear. José laughs. Not for long, I guarantee. I hope none of you three have a temper. If you do, try and lose it somewhere if you can, and don't go looking for it again. Lose it with a Protestant and have done with it. There must be plenty of those in England. I have to say, we missed your mama's singing. Guaxara is a good soprano, but I like a little more meat. A lot more! Your mama has a wonderful voice. Make sure you ask her to teach you to sing like her. She must be very popular in London.*"

"I didn't know Mama could sing," said Carmen.

"She can't. It is Grandmamma's wishful thinking. Old people do that. They get to a stage when they believe that their thoughts are real."

"Grandmamma may be right," suggested Tessa. "We're too far away to know if her thoughts are real or not."

"Have you heard Mama sing?"

TESSA RETURNED TO her labels. There was something missing, but she didn't know what. They looked like a young girl's first cologne instead of a sophisticated woman's perfumes lining a dressing table. She continued to paint carefully, *Corsica Flora*.

Mariquita didn't finish the letter. She folded it, slotted the two sheets back into the envelope and thrust it into her pocket.

CARMEN FORGOT TO insist on knowing whether their mother could really sing or to ask what the bride's dress was like or whether the bride loved the groom. She swirled her vivid brush across the page, unconcerned that they had a host of relatives in Spain she would never meet.

MARIQUITA WATCHED HER younger sisters from her chair. She had no desire to join them. She knew she would clear up the dirty jar of water and wash out the brushes when they had finished. She would throw away Carmen's paintings, and as they crumpled in her hands, the thick paint would crack through the daubed layers. Carmen never asked about her discarded works of art because it was the doing that mattered, right there, in the moment, and she would create others anew, another day.

Tessa was different. She would put her creations on the shelf above her bed and forbid anyone else from touching them, even when the labels curled, the paint faded and the liquid dried grey against the glass.

IN JEREZ DE la Frontera, the Garcia relatives and their friends sat on the shaded terrace and continued to dissect the wedding day. It had been a success, as are all weddings in the heat of southern Spain. The crickets provided the music now that it was over, and the old women sat and thought of their supple youth, whilst the old men smoked and thought of the harvest. All of them tried not to think of the price they had paid.

Chapter Four

T HAT EVENING, MR. Garcia introduced his wife to his accountant, Mr. Jackson, and Mr. Jackson's wife. They stood in the drawing room before the roaring fire, sipping warm Garcia sherry from Jerez de la Frontera.

Although business was not spoken of, Mr. Garcia warmed to the description of the hot vineyards he had been brought up in as a child. Although he never said that he yearned to return, Mr. Jackson knew his client was a foreigner on unfamiliar soil and that he would be relied upon to guide his client through any English eccentricities.

On occasions such as this, Mrs. Garcia did not wish she were elsewhere as she often did: she once again became Ann Loughlin, the girl with the resounding alto voice and the swing to her hips, who had been born at sea as her father captained the ship. An Irish girl in London, she never felt as though she was a foreigner. This was perhaps because she relived her past life as though it were the present. She had also travelled across most of the world before reaching the age of five.

So while her husband spoke of the crackling sun and the ancient wood casks with their soft, smoky aromas, she glittered with universal laughter and was happy exactly where she stood, on the darkly patterned rug.

UPSTAIRS, IN MRS. Garcia's bedroom, Tessa sat on the long, upholstered stool at her mother's dressing table and held a bottle up to the gentle glow of the lamp and declared which perfume she liked best. Mariquita sat beside her.

"Put that down," she ordered before levering the bottle from her sister's fingers and replacing it on the lace cloth.

The dressing table was Mrs. Garcia's second-favourite place in the house, after her bed, but it was Tessa's favourite.

ONCE MRS. GARCIA had risen from under the sheets, blankets and eiderdown, she would sit on the long, upholstered stool and stare into the mirror. She did not always see Mrs. Garcia. Frequently, she saw Ann Loughlin. She did not burst into song on these occasions, but into tears. Due to the noise and activity of the house, nobody ever heard her. Left in solitude, she would brush her auburn hair, and no matter how many times she ran the bristles down, her hair remained strong. It fanned out, waving goodbye as it journeyed from her scalp. She didn't know when she had grown old. When had the tiny fissures above her top lip first appeared? When had the solitary line between her eyes deepened? When had her pink skin lost its bloom?

She wondered if her childhood sweetheart would look at her kindly, and she stroked her cheek, recalling the touch of his hand. Would he be glad that he had eventually married a girl who had stayed in the town where their parents had been born and knew everyone he knew? Did he miss her? Did he ever sit by an open window on a summer evening and walk with her down the lane? Patrick Murray. She wondered what his lips would feel like now they were old. She wondered if they would still be soft and warm. Her sweet, sweet Patrick. She had chosen other lips and another life. *Another life. That is what it had really been about*, she told herself while she hung in the web that had woven around her.

Casting away these thoughts, she touched the array of perfume bottles on the dressing table to remind herself of moments in their marriage. She noted how the bottles had grown more ornate as the years passed. Jewellery had accumulated too. She fingered the pearl necklace in its velvet box and recalled the expression on her father-in-law's face as he looked at her from the top of the stairs before keeling over and tumbling down as an iron wrench gripped his heart. "A family trait," they said as they threw orange flowers onto the coffin and watched parched soil splatter the wooden box. The lace cloth that now covered her dressing table had been a present when they left Spain for England the following year. She missed her husband's family for their meals at long tables on the terrace, for their doors swung open to whoever called and stayed all day. She missed singing at the end of an evening and falling asleep in the large, white bed with the shutters holding out the insects, and her husband holding her in his arms. She missed rolling away from his breath and feeling the hot night on her face. And now, rather than sing, she dabbed perfume on her throat.

Tessa picked up another of her mother's perfume bottles and turned it to the light.

"Put it down," pleaded Mariquita. "Let's go to the kitchen and ask Cook if there are any desserts left. Come on. Be a sweet pea."

"I like this one best."

"Me too. Come on now."

Tessa held the bottle close to Mariquita's eyes. "What can you see?"

"Blue. Purple. Pink."

"I can see mermaids."

Tessa pulled the stopper and held it out to Mariquita, who leant forward to smell it. Tessa wrinkled her face.

"You don't smell it like that. Here." She pressed the stopper against Mariquita's neck. "You have to know what to do."

"Why?"

"For when you meet the person that made this."

Mariquita pushed Tessa's hand away. "This is all nonsense. I detest perfume. Sherry is what is important."

Tessa waved the stopper in the air.

"You only say that because our papa makes sherry, but now you know Mister François Coty makes perfume, you'll realise it is as important, if not more, in fact."

"Papa doesn't make the sherry. Uncle Juan does. Papa *imports* it."

"It's our name on the crates."

"It's the family name."

"Mr. Coty does both. I want to do both. I'll be the head of the entire family exactly like him."

"Don't be disrespectful. Papa is the head."

"I mean when I grow up. When I have a profession."

"Papa will still be the head and you… Put those down. It's time for your bed."

"I'll try this last one."

She reached for the blue bottle as Mariquita reached to stop her, and a few drops of liquid spotted Tessa's nightgown. They both stared at the oily circles on the white cotton before Mariquita put the bottle down with too much force. Tessa fell to the floor as she fumbled to retrieve the bee-like stopper that had rolled under the lace cloth.

"Give it here!"

At that moment, the door handle turned. They looked up as the door swung open and Mrs. Garcia in her blue evening gown swept into the room.

Immersed in their conversation, they hadn't heard the front door close behind the well-dined accountant and his wife, or their mother's footsteps on the creaking stair.

The stopper stung Tessa's palm. Mariquita rose to her feet. Mrs. Garcia stared at them both. White sparks flashed in her eyes, but her voice remained calm.

"Get out," she said.

The girls stumbled towards the landing, jostling against each other to be the first to leave.

"Not you."

Mariquita froze. Tessa paused in the doorway. Mariquita held out her arm and, touching her sister's hand briefly, the hard, cold stopper passed from one to the other.

18

Later, when Tessa could not sleep, she looked for her elder sister where she knew she would find her. After moments of contact with the storm, Mariquita always took refuge in the place her mother would never enter. Tessa found her sister standing in their wardrobe. They stared at each other for a moment before Tessa quietly closed the door again.

Chapter Five

A FTER THE INITIAL September morning nip, the air swelled warm and pulsed with stewed apple and mulched blackberries. A small biplane hung in the blue sky. From the pavement, ten-year-old Alfonso gazed upwards. Older by two years, Frank feigned nonchalance; he could not understand how it stayed in the air. He knew that a bird had hollow bones, rendering it light enough to fly. He suspected that a man's bones were not like a bird's because when he had fallen out of the horse-chestnut tree, he had plummeted like a full barrel of sherry, so how was it possible a metal structure could stay in the sky?

"What is it?" asked Tessa.

"It's Roe! I'm sure it is," said Alfonso.

"Who?"

"Wave! D'you think he can see us?"

"If he comes down, he will," said Frank.

They craned to see as the aircraft puttered beyond the chimneystacks.

Alfonso caught Tessa looking at him.

"What?"

She grinned at her favourite brother.

Mrs. Garcia did not break her stride as she picked up speed. "It'll end with broken bodies on the streets."

Their mother had eventually risen from her bed as the tailor was making the final alterations for the boys' school clothes and she felt a purpose in her limbs.

"Will there be a lot of blood if it hits the pavement?" Frank asked. "I don't like blood."

"Louis Bleriot is the best," announced Alfonso.

"Is he the one who has the pixie engine?" Tessa asked.

"Gnome. It's a Gnome engine."

"I don't see the difference. They're both really small."

"It's high up there," Joseph said. "It's a long way away. That's why it's small."

"I can see that."

"Tessa knows," said Alfonso.

"The French are the best at everything," Tessa agreed.

Uproar broke out.

"What about the Irish?" demanded Mariquita.

"The Spanish, more to the point!" argued Joseph.

Alfonso shouted the loudest. "Tessa's right! No-one beats the French for engineering."

"The Americans?"

"No-one beats the English at anything."

No-one heard Frank.

Mariquita walked close to their mother, admiring of her purpose and unaware that her mother's speed was driven by an attempt to create space between them.

"Boys! Come on. You don't want Mr. Bridgeman to have gone home and closed the shop," she called over her shoulder, looking for approval from the place it would never come.

Mrs. Garcia had long since stopped wondering why she disliked her eldest daughter. At fifteen, she was already taller, broader and hairier than herself. Dark, downy hairs shadowed her upper lip. Her eyebrows met in the middle, and she walked without charm. She could not dance, sing or play the piano. More importantly, she had not the imagination to invent excuses as to why not. Unconsciously, Mrs. Garcia had come to rely on these very deficiencies because they freed Mariquita to take up the role of housekeeper and herself to disappear. There was nothing Mariquita liked more than to open the doors of the well-arranged linen press, and nothing her mother liked more than to let her. Neither realised it, but they had the perfect working relationship.

At the corner of the street, Mrs. Garcia turned to ascertain that they would all cross the road as one, and Mariquita stumbled against her, making familiar nauseous growth swirl in her stomach. Although she rarely took any of the children out, she recalled the rising sense of panic as though it were an hourly occurrence.

In the distance, Frank was talking to a tall gentleman whilst stroking his Airedale terrier. Slightly closer, Alfonso and Joseph strolled as though they had until Christmas to discuss the merits of French aviation over that of the English or American. Tessa gazed into a shop window.

"Hurry up," Mrs. Garcia called.

Straightening her hat, Mariquita grasped her opportunity and strode swiftly back along the pavement. Taking hold of Frank's right arm, she pulled him away from the wiry-haired dog. En route, she hastened Joseph and Alfonso in front of her and swept Tessa away from the shop window. She moved them all towards her mother like leaves caught in the current down to the estuary. Mrs. Garcia didn't acknowledge her success but turned and stepped off the kerb.

They followed, but as they reached the other pavement, Mariquita smelt an imminent threat. Her nostrils began to tremble, her eyes to stab and prickle as though scratched by thorns, and her nose threatened to explode like a seedpod. She sniffed then held her breath. Finally, she sneezed.

"Bless you," said Joseph.

Tessa glanced frantically about until she saw the woman. Mrs. Garcia had seen her too and approached a display of multicoloured roses. "Are they fresh?"

The woman looked battle weary. Her colourful troops gathered close around her, and she eyed them with ill-disguised contempt.

"Fresh as the dew, ma'am. How many'll it be?"

"Half a dozen."

No-one spoke of the boxes of flowers from Covent Garden that filled the kitchen table every week. Joseph stepped forward, arms outstretched.

"Hand them to your sister. With a little luck, she won't crush them," said Mrs. Garcia.

Without a word, Joseph placed the flowers in Mariquita's arms.

She looked at him through watery eyes. He sighed and shrugged while she sneezed in reply.

TESSA HAD ONLY come with them because her shop was en route to the tailor's. She knew they wouldn't be allowed inside the chemist shop, but she hoped to peer through the window. The boys were still gazing skywards, and Frank was being Frank and talking to strangers, so she grasped the opportunity, stopped and gazed through the window of Juniper and Company. Everything before her glowed reddish brown, including the dancing figures of the Fates, with their wild hair and long robes fixed on the richly coloured glass bottles. Her eyes travelled from the flower-holding figures to the words, *L'Ambre Antique*. Above the bottles and boxes and draping fabrics and the cards depicting the Fates, curled the name she sought. She mouthed it out loud.

"François Coty."

Leaning forward, her nose touched the glass. She pushed it, trying to reach the rich, warm velvet and smell the aroma held in the gleaming flacons. One day, when she was older, she would enter the shop through the front door and point to one of the bottles on display and purchase her very own perfume. She whispered it—

"L'Ambre Antique."

—mesmerised by the image of herself as a grown woman, until her nose bruised against the window as Mariquita shoved her along the pavement. Alfonso caught her arms and, spanning them wide, propelled her forwards as if together, they were a double-winged aircraft, skimming the earth.

Chapter Six

THREE YEARS LATER, when all the boys except Joseph and Frank were once again returning to school, Tessa watched from an upstairs window. Splatters of rain marked the glass, fracturing her brothers into blurred shapes so that they progressed with jerking movements from the house to a black car.

IN ANOTHER ROOM, a bee-shaped stopper of A Coeur des Calices lay on the dressing table. Listening to the raindrops, Mrs. Garcia placed the stopper back into the neck of the bottle and released a long-held breath.

THE CAR HAVING gone, Tessa crept past her mother's closed door, stepped over the creaking stair and retrieved the afternoon post from the metal cage before tiptoeing down the hallway to her father's study. She tapped gently, and went inside without waiting, shutting the door against the piano music emanating from the breakfast room. Sitting opposite her father, she sliced open an envelope with the silver knife and took out a sheet of paper. She glanced at the signature before handing it across the desk.

"Captain Hatchett from the bank."

Slice.

"Mr. Jackson. Numbers as usual."

Mr. Garcia nodded. She held out a thick sheet of paper and as she did so noticed he looked tired.

"This is from Grandmamma."

Mr. Garcia continued to read the letter in his hand. "Take it to your mother. She will read it to me later."

"I can read it to you."

"Not now."

Tessa reached across and picked a Liquorice Allsort out of a paper bag. They looked at each other. The piano sounded its discord.

"Couldn't you have sent Carmen to school as well?" she asked.

Mr. Garcia smiled. "Have another."

A few hours later, the three Garcia girls sat close together on a wooden pew in the church where they'd been baptised, waiting for their turn to confess. It was late in the day. There would be no-one confessing after them.

"Father Ryan is going to think it's Christmas and Easter all rolled into one when he hears what I have to tell him," Carmen announced, her voice bright in the musty silence.

They watched a blonde-haired boy leave the confessional box, and Carmen filled his place faster than a plummeting rag doll. The curtain hadn't stopped swinging when they heard her announce in her proud voice.

"I feel *bad*!"

Mariquita moved across to the side altar and Tessa reluctantly followed. She was tired. She wanted to sit still, but the expanse of her sister's back wouldn't let her.

"It's a *huge* sin, isn't it? Isn't it?"

Carmen's tone was as full of discord as her piano playing.

"I don't want to go back to the convent," said Mariquita. "I'm too old."

"I don't want to go either."

"One more year."

"Then Carmen will descend on the nuns."

"And I'll be at home."

"Why don't you ask Papa if you can go to Jerez instead?"

"Because I want to come home. Mama needs me."

Tessa glanced at her elder sister's profile. She had never seen her excited or angry or happy. She was always solid and protective and unavoidable.

"Are you *sure* it isn't a sin?" Carmen's voice sliced through the wooden pews, the porcelain statues, gold candlesticks and flower displays.

"Tell her she's finished and bring her out," Mariquita said without looking at her sister. "It's your turn."

Tessa took Carmen's reluctantly released seat in the dark confessional. The priest's breath growled on the other side of the screen, but Carmen's words still rang out between them.

"Mariquita doesn't miss them a scrap," Carmen had said. "She says she's glad our brothers have gone back to school because it's less work for her. If I feel bad about them going and it's not a sin, then it must be a sin if she feels good about it. Are you going to punish her? Are you? What are you going to make her do?"

Tessa stared straight ahead to where the priest waited for her confession. It didn't seem to matter what you said, she decided, when it appeared to be a random decision whether feelings were considered good or not.

"I don't want to be a mother when I grow up," she declared.

"Our Lady was a mother."

"She didn't have a choice."

FATHER RYAN WATCHED the three Garcia girls leave. He wondered how the priest at the Covent School in Belgium would answer them. It had been a long day and they had silenced him. It was always the ones who sinned the least who bothered him. He rubbed the round of his empty stomach and hastened past the carnations to the vestry. He could almost taste the shepherd's pie that was bubbling as it hardened at the edges on the middle shelf of the oven.

IN THE FOLLOWING years, during the holidays, when she returned from Maeseyck, Tessa continued to act as her father's secretary. It did not cross her mind to wonder who opened his mail and read his letters and typed his replies when she was away. All that mattered was that it was she who watched and waited for instructions while he strode backwards and forwards over the rug in front of his father's portrait. It was even better when he popped a sweet into his mouth because then she would use her initiative to decipher his words. And then he'd give the go-ahead, and she'd sit importantly at the big Corona machine and type.

"In future, I wish you to deal directly with my accountant, Mr. Jackson of Clapham. He is acquainted with all my directions and we feel it best that he converses with you on all matters concerning The Garcia Corporation for the Importation of Fine Wine and Sherries."

Tessa's fingers paused on the keys.

"Are you sure about this, Papa? Mr. Coty deals with all his business himself. He doesn't trust anyone else to do it."

"You have to trust other people," said Mr. Garcia. "Where would I be if I didn't trust Joseph at the warehouse with the arrival of the crates from Jerez?"

"Joseph and I are family."

"Mr. Jackson is an accountant. You have to trust those who are experts in their field."

"I suppose so, but don't you want to know what he says? Mr. Coty keeps an eye on everyone he gives a job to."

"Your Mr. Coty will wear himself out."

"Isn't it best to know exactly what people do? After all, it's you they are speaking for."

"Allow me to run my business as I see fit."

"I'm not telling you what to do, Papa."

"Give me that letter to sign."

Tessa extracted the typed sheet, and her father signed it with his dark-red fountain pen.

"You may address the envelope and seal it."

"Do I get two Liquorice Allsorts for following your orders?"

He nodded. Distracted. She reached for the white paper bag.

"Papa! There are none left!"

The expression on Mr. Garcia's face drained to bewilderment.

"Ask Mariquita to purchase some more when she is out, will you?"

TESSA THOUGHT IT was extraordinary her father had let his supply of sweets run out. However, for Mr. Garcia, it was merely something else at odds with the day. He couldn't pin down exactly what it was that rumbled like a distant avalanche, but so far, there seemed no need to run through the house, calling for everyone to evacuate. Sometimes, sitting still was the better option, so Mr. Garcia sent Tessa to ask Mariquita to buy another bag of his favourite sweets and confided his unease to no-one, and nobody else noticed the faint tremors of increasing unease brought by the postman each day.

AS USUAL, AT the end of the week, Tessa, still unaware, gathered the daily pile of letters in preparation for their delivery to the post office. This had become her favourite task, as it was proof of what she had done and been allowed to do, for her father.

"Is that the lot?" she asked, halfway across the room towards the door.

As her father made no reply, she repeated the question, before turning to check that he had heard.

"Papa?"

Mr. Garcia leant forward in his chair as if caught in the act of rising to his feet. His eyes fixed on her as if they were trying to tell her something. Normally, on his asking for her assistance, she would have rushed to his side, but on this occasion, his rigidity held her static. She stared back at him, staring at her, and waited for him to tell her what was on his mind, behind those pleading eyes. After a few moments, though, his taut body relaxed, the intensity in his eyes softened, and he leaned back down into his chair.

"Is this the lot?" she asked, waving the envelopes, unsure of what had happened but knowing that something momentous had taken place.

Chapter Seven

AT EIGHTEEN, MARIQUITA already looked and acted like a middle-aged woman, from her spreading feet, through her broad hips, to her hairy top lip. And she believed, based on fact rather than pride, that her family would not survive one day without her. From the minute she rose until the hour she retired to bed, she moulded the Garcia household into her own vision of how it should be.

No-one could alter Mariquita's beliefs. The nuns had not pierced her soul by suggesting humility, and she had returned from the convent at the start of the war with an unaltered confidence in her position in the Garcia household. She remained the same child she had always been, but in adult form. Her parents had both, in their own ways, failed to engage her, and everyone silently agreed that it was best to leave the eldest Garcia girl to her own devices.

So, in the morning, when breakfast had been cleared, she was the one who spoke to Cook about the day's meals. It was she who took it upon herself to organise a tempting tray to be taken to her mother's room should Mrs. Garcia seem disposed to remain there. During the school holidays, she planned the morning's studies for her sisters, who rarely accomplished a quarter of what was asked of them. She never wavered but nor did she aim to be a schoolteacher. The convent would sort them out soon, whenever it was their turn, although she did suspect that school had little use in the real world. In the between times, she tied her two sisters up with time.

The only grain of sand rubbing in her hourglass was Mr. Garcia. She knew what was in the hearts of all members of the household, except his. She knew her mother remained in bed, hating London smog. She knew Carmen wanted to create bedlam rather than socks, that Tessa yearned to type rather than knit scarves, that Joseph would rather move counters on a map than be a counter in a trench, and Frank dreamt of waving a hockey stick once more. Ensconced in Spain, she knew that Nacho would be whispering and Tony shouting. That Alfonso watched the sky, while Matty had his feet firmly on the ground. She knew them all. It was a fact. She, Mariquita Garcia y Diaz, positioned them like her individual army and kept them all in their respective bunkers. However, she was increasingly aware that her father was absent without leave. Her only hold on him was the steady supply of Liquorice Allsorts, and she had no intention of relinquishing her charge on the supply chain.

No-one in the house understood, but no-one questioned her mission to make an ally of her mother. Mariquita herself was unaware of what was really going on, behind the rigid control she enforced. She laid her mother's meal trays herself, carefully pressing a cloth she had embroidered and smoothing it gently over the wood. She polished the cutlery until it gleamed, ensured that the water in the crystal jug was ice cold and that the drinking glass shone. She placed food on the plate, carefully regarding the rations, not so much as to be over-facing, not so little as to be stingy. She arranged the morning letters, or a flower or note with care, and she carried it up the stairs herself, to her mother's door on the frontline, and it was her knuckles that tapped the wood. Perhaps she should have waited for her mother's order to advance, but she did not suppose that the supplies or her presence would be unwelcome. She would venture into what she considered friendly territory and drop the legs of the tray, placing them over her mother's thighs and so pinning her to the bed. She would receive no thanks, but she expected none, taking her mother's gratitude instead from the empty plates.

It was Abigail who discreetly disposed of the discarded food in the bin and who silently cursed the mistress for the wastage of the carefully prepared tray, and the daughter for her unceasing devotion.

On the other hand, Mariquita did not court her father's affections. She ran his house as a general, and there was satisfaction enough in that. With an assurance that he would always provide for her, she played her part in their small army, merely desiring that the sergeants and privates did the same.

It was only in church that, although her mind planned and made decisions, she remained physically inactive. In church, she clasped her hands and prayed for Joseph and Frank. She prayed that Joseph was eating well, that he kept his uniform clean and that he replied to her letters. Like hers to him, they were factual and robustly cheerful.

She prayed that Frank would be able to sleep through the night without coughing, and that he would look out of the window without crying. She prayed that the soups she served him would take away the pallor from his skin. She prayed to see him play ice hockey again in December, but she did not put her hands together for anyone else. She felt that the others were all capable of praying for themselves, and if they didn't, then they would reap the consequences. When she had finished her prayers, which she said as soon as she sat on a front pew, she always looked up to gaze with contempt at the alabaster figure of Mary.

It wasn't that she didn't like Mary, merely this version of Mary. Even if she did like this Mary, she still wouldn't have directed her prayers to her. She had found out long ago that if a prayer was worth saying, it was worth going directly to the highest-ranking officer. In no circumstances would she call on a subordinate. She needed answers there and then, and a second-in-command did not have sufficient authority. So she sat and studied this woman who had been chosen by God, and she wondered why. She'd had this thought for as long as she could remember and had never been able to fathom it out. At one time, she had merely accepted it. After all, Mary was the perfect soldier. But after a time, the old doubt had resurfaced, and it had been stronger than ever before. She knew deep down in her bones that this plaster cast Virgin was not worthy. The chalky-coloured figure was not deserving of all the adoration it received. One autumnal afternoon, surrounded by chrysanthemums, she realised why.

Mary was not pink and white and frail like this statue. The Madonna was brown and dark and strong. She was big and hard-working. She was tough. That was why God had chosen her. He knew she would survive. What would be the point in her giving birth to a baby if she collapsed and died at the end of it because she was too delicate? No. Mary had to be robust. Mary had to be black-haired and brown-skinned because she lived in a hot country. Mary had to be like her, Mariquita, born in the heat, fuelled with the stamina of a heavy woman and with the constitution of an Amazonian.

That late September afternoon, Mariquita felt as though a trap door from heaven had opened and the light shone down on her. She would gratefully remain a virgin like Mary because it meant that she too was chosen. She rose from her pedestal and smiled in pity at the plaster statue that was not Mary, and from that day was secure in the knowledge that she was the personification of the Virgin wherever she travelled in the deceived Western world.

Chapter Eight

My darling Tessa,

I hope you are in good health and continuing to enjoy your studies despite all that is happening in Europe. Please know that we are assured of your safety at the convent and are confident of the care you have there. Your mama rightly reminded me that during wartime, nowhere could be safer than with the nuns we all know and trust. She is mostly cross that the Germans think they can interrupt your schooling rather than any of the other damage the war has done. Of course, it will not be long before you are home again, and we are pleased that will be so.

I hope you remember this and use your time well, perfecting your French, which I know you think I worry about too much, but believe me, it will stand you in good stead.

News here: Frank is still a little out of sorts, but Mariquita has worked out a regime to get him back on his feet, and Joseph will be with us shortly. We had a glowing letter from his captain. It didn't sound like our Pepe at all, to be frank, so I ripped it up. But that is only between you and me. Can't have a stranger harping on about selflessness like that. Must have him mixed up with someone else! Your mama wouldn't read it.

The weather's not been too bright. Too much fog. That's the least of our worries, I know, but it does get your mama down. Not much has changed in our four walls with this dreadful war, except for poor Frank. Anyway, you'll see that soon enough for yourself.

Please give Carmen a kiss and of course the same for you.

Affectionately yours,
Papa.

x

THAT NIGHT, AS Europe learnt how to breathe again, Tessa lay in her bed in the Convent des Ursulines and dreamt of the French perfumier, François Coty, glad he had survived the war unscathed. She dreamt of him not as the great man of perfume, but as the little boy whose name had been François Spoturno.

Instinctively, she heard the quiet of his life. She imagined how, with both parents dead, his grandmother used to spoil him and let him sleep next to her warm body and how she waved to him from the doorway as he ran out to play. How Tessa envied him those fields as opposed to hard pavements and flagged churches. She ran with him, feeling the grass on their bare legs, holding his small hand as he pointed to the pine trees for her to smell. They knelt together and rubbed their fingers against the leaves of marjoram, thyme and mint. They sniffed each other's fingertips and ran across the grass where they breathed in the scents of mimosa and wild jasmine.

In the classroom, she sat beside him, marvelling at how advanced he was in his studies, only to stand when the doors were closed to him because his grandmamma, Anna-Maria, decided there were better ways to learn. Together, they made a pledge, blown by the wind under the fragrant pine trees, that they would conquer the world. Like his hero, Napoleon, Coty declared he would, and why would she not believe him? And if he could do it, why not she?

They would never forget their cry to battle amongst the wild hills of Corsica.

Dear Tessa,

Hang it all, the war would have to end before I got a chance to join in! I could have been bombing German cities with the Royal Air Force (Royal Flying Corps to you), instead of sitting in a stifling classroom. I hate being stuck here in southern Spain, miles from anything remotely interesting. I'll just have to spice up what Joseph and Frank have to say. How is Frank? Is his chest any better? Have to ask him how much that gas stank. Talking of stink, Tony's been making stink bombs. Not very popular with the priests, I can tell you! But it was funny. We had to evacuate the whole west wing for a week. Marvellous! Don't tell Tony I said that. Young fellow is bigheaded enough already.

Tell me what you're up to, say hello to Carmen. Release is nigh, don't you know?

Love Alfonso x

Dear Papa,

Thank you for your letter. I have kept them all in a box under my bed, and I re-read them frequently. I start to read them to Carmen, but she only wants an edited version.

I, on the other hand, like to read about how you're feeling and what you're thinking as well as what you're doing. I wish you'd include more of that. Your letters can never be long enough, and you still haven't said how you're managing without me. I suppose you're writing your letters in longhand as you used to. You do have beautiful handwriting. I love to receive your letters, so I can easily understand that your bank manager and Mr. Jackson think likewise, though I don't suppose you need to write to Mr. Jackson very often.

The food is dreadful. Well, not dreadful. Bland. The vegetable gardens have been replanted, but I think we'd all like a little more meat. Rabbit stew is pretty tasteless, and it would be nice to have a change. But that is selfish when all food for Frank must taste funny. Please tell him to get well soon and give him kisses from Carmen and myself.

I hope Mama is well and that you are too, and that Joseph returns without falling over anything. I'm glad you burned the letter they sent about him. I hate it when people think they know your family better than you do yourself, and insist on telling you so. You're absolutely right. Our Joseph isn't selfless. By saying that he is, they're showing themselves up as the impostors they really are. Sister Anne does it all the time. She's always saying how I remind her of Mariquita. I look nothing like her! I don't think Carmen looks like her either. None of us looks alike, but all the nuns say, "Ah! You Garcia girls! All as alike as peas in a pod." And our personalities? Don't get me started on that. I don't know what kind of peas they grow in Belgium, but they're definitely not Spanish peas.

I'll write again soon. I have to go. Evensong is bellowing!

Love and much affection,
Tessa

x

TESSA NEVER STAYED long at evensong. In her mind, as the sun set behind the stained glass in the chapel, she stepped off the boat at Marseilles and stood on the dock beside François Spoturno. They both stared at the steamships sliding between the forts at the harbour entrance, at the sails and masts moving with the swell and at the nets drying. The crew had been kind on the journey from Corsica, but she and he were the only children. In the months to follow, she watched over François' shoulder as he grew up, learning to banter with the sailors, pimps and ship owners. She joined him as he sold lace and moiré ribbon to the fancy goods shops of the port. They competed with each other to spot a naturally elegant woman from an impostor, and little by little, they developed a sense of good taste.

"Don't leave me!" she wanted to shout. "Don't replace me!"

But he did; of course he did. Tessa recognised ambition and his need to conquer the world. She let go of his hand and waved to him as he journeyed to Paris. He'd have no time for her when he began climbing the ladder to success.

SHE STARED AT the stained glass of the altar window in the chapel at the Convent des Ursulines in Belgium and watched him gaze in wonder at the beautiful Lalique glassware on display at the Great Exhibition in Paris.

"We'll meet again," she whispered. "When I'm grown up, we'll meet again, François Coty."

Chapter Nine

SEEING THE POSTMAN crossing the street as she arrived home, Tessa quickened her pace. It was comforting to see the familiar uniform and ritual and to know daily life had continued during her final term in Belgium and that she was ready to climb her own ladder to success.

"Good morning! Are those letters for us?"

The postman was not the accustomed Mr. Brookes, and he refused to release the envelopes in his hand.

"Garcia?" she said. "I'll take them and the parcel. I'm Miss Teresa Garcia."

"Sorry, Miss, can't do that. Not regulation, and I could lose my job."

He hurried up the steps, leaving her on the pavement. The sound of the door knocker roared down the street. She bounded after him, swinging her holdall, but he stared at the door, refusing to catch her eye. When the door remained closed, he raised the lower lip of the brass lion again.

"I do live here," she insisted.

In the confusion of the door opening, her bag brushing the postman's leg and the passing of envelopes and parcel, she didn't get the chance to prove her point. The postman tottered down the steps, and the door began to close. Just in time, she held out her hand.

A pale woman stood there, irritation shadowing her face.

"How do you do?" Tessa said. "May I come in?"

The woman held the post more tightly. The paper on the package crackled.

"I'm sorry, who are you?" The woman drew herself up. "Are you here to see Mrs. Garcia?"

"No! I'm the second daughter of the house. Teresa Garcia."

The woman tightened her jaw. "My apologies, Miss Garcia. I'm sure you understand my hesitance as we have not met before," she said, raising her chin. "I am Miss Havers, Mr. Garcia's assistant. I was told you weren't due home until the end of July, and so I did not expect you." She peered down the steps. "You are alone?"

Tessa nodded. "Carmen wasn't in the hurry I was."

It was then that they shook hands. Glancing over Miss Havers' shoulder, Tessa glimpsed a figure moving slowly towards them.

"Papa?"

Miss Havers stepped aside to allow Tessa to enter the house, and dropping her bag, she flung her arms around her father. Under her embrace, she felt his bones through the jacket and smelt the stale smell of tobacco.

MR. GARCIA COULD not remember why this daughter loved him so much, only that she must do, to embrace him so hard. If his chest didn't feel so empty, he felt sure he must love her equally. In the shaded hall, he held this young woman because he yearned for the child she had been and that time when he deserved to be central to her world.

SHROUDED IN HER own hopes, she put the reason that her father's shoulders were thinner than they had been, and that his wrists had become almost as slim as her own, to the fact that his work had been more difficult without her and this Miss Havers didn't know his habits and needs. She pulled back before he did, her face full of smiles.

"All will be well now," she assured him.

Clutching the morning's post, Miss Havers nodded briefly to Mr. Garcia and with measured steps retraced her way to the study.

"You are home for good?"

"Yes, Papa, and ready to start work at once. You can tell Miss Havers that you don't need her anymore. Perhaps I should start tomorrow rather than right now. Give her a chance to find a new position."

"What are you talking about? You've only this minute stepped through the door."

"I know, Papa. I know, but I'm so excited to start. I've been thinking and planning, and I have so much to talk to you about. I have a strategy that will bring Garcia sherry into every household in England."

"Strategy?"

"My hours will need to be defined, and we need to decide where I will sit in your study or if we want to be based here or at the warehouse. I was thinking about that on the train, and I think that clients would prefer—"

"I like my study!"

"So do I!" She laughed.

"Tessa. Calm down. Let me call the others. Ann? Mariquita? Ann?"

She took hold of her father's hand. "I'm so glad to be back. All will be well now."

"All is well." He shuffled a few steps down the hall. "Your mother will be pleased to see you."

And then he left her. Walked away, following Miss Havers to the study and closing the door behind him.

For one moment, the house held its breath as she stood alone in the dark hallway. The mirror on the wall would not look at her. A rose petal fell onto the polished walnut of the hall table. Then doors began opening, footsteps walking, running. Voices. Noise. The familiar sounds of the house.

"Tessa?"

Frank stood at the top of the stairs. Tall, thin Frank with his skin tinged by the trenches. Mariquita loomed out of the dining room. Abigail followed, flour brushed across her face and then arms around her and hers around them and kisses and questions and the sight of her mother floating down the stairs.

"So, you're back," Mrs. Garcia said.

AT BREAKFAST THE next morning, when Tessa rose to fetch the post, Mariquita placed a hand on her arm and told her that she didn't need to do that anymore. Sharp footsteps clicked along the hallway.

Alfonso winked at her. "You've been replaced, sis."

She stuck out her tongue and hurried from the room with the taste of honey lingering in her mouth, only to see Miss Havers struggling to open the wire cage and retrieve the post. Seizing her moment, Tessa sped down the hall and entered the study without knocking. Her father sat in his chair. The sound of the cage rattling reached into the room. Tessa closed the door.

"Good morning, Papa."

"Good morning. What may I do for you?"

"Why does Miss Havers feel she needs to collect the post?"

"That's her job."

"But she's leaving today."

Panic flashed over his eyes. "Why? What's happened?"

"Nothing. Only I thought Miss Havers would have gathered her things and be preparing to leave, not—"

Mr. Garcia rose to his feet. "Why would she do that?"

Tessa flinched at the discord in his voice. She glanced at the door. The cage no longer rattled.

"Because you'll have told her to?" She spoke uneasily. "We agreed. You don't need her now that I have come home."

"We agreed nothing."

"Don't worry, Papa, I can type. I speak excellent French now—it's good you made me stick with it. I'm organised, and my spelling is good. Did you read the report from the nuns?" She tried to make her voice calming and unrushed even though her heart beat fast.

"You did well, but I did not insist on you studying French so that you would be my assistant. You are a young lady now. Those are your accomplishments, and now that you are home, you have other duties to fulfil."

"But I've always helped you. I thought it was agreed I would be your assistant."

"I didn't think for a moment that you were serious."

"Of course I was serious! Weren't you?"

The door opened. Mr. Garcia physically relaxed.

"Good morning."

Tessa jumped at the sound of Miss Havers' voice.

"Let's get started," Mr. Garcia said, sitting back down. "Tessa? If you'll excuse us, we must start our day."

Chapter Ten

Tessa stood in the nursery, not knowing what to do. She had studied and planned how her life would be. Leave the convent when she reached eighteen, work as her father's secretary, take over the running of various aspects of the business, alongside Joseph. Set up an importing arm in Paris. Become a well-respected businesswoman and meet François Coty. Logical steps. Yet before she'd begun, the first rung had been snapped from under her feet.

All those years of preparation seemed like a waste. She no longer understood the sense in learning to read and write in French, to know what to say and when and why forgiveness was so important. She thought back over the futile days studying arithmetic, when she was not allowed to keep accounts. She wondered if the nuns knew of the pretence.

She cried not only for herself, but for her friends, feeling their disappointment that their dreams, like hers, would not come to fruition. She recalled their eager faces that held no inkling that their parents and teachers knew they had no futures in the working world. She wondered how she would warn Carmen in a way she'd believe. How could she tell her that her passion for horticulture would come to nothing? How to tell her that spending a summer at the convent to learn the difference in planting carrots and artichokes would not lead to her running her own vegetable-growing business?

Mrs. Garcia walked out of the room as soon as she raised her voice in protest. Mr. Garcia hid behind his study door. Miss Havers appeared to be as fixed in the house as the floorboards and the boys, all of them, out of the house all day, unaware and unreachable. Worst of all, Mariquita loomed like a battleship in every doorway. After the first battery of words, Tessa didn't know what to say to anyone anymore, so she fell silent and withdrew into her own thoughts. Minutes passed, hours, days merging one into the next.

One weekend, Alfonso, noticing her slumping around the house, took her with him to the coast, with two friends in their automobile. The beach spread almost empty before them, and they paddled in the shallows, avoiding broken mussels and delicate crab skeletons. She lifted her face to the passing clouds and breathed in freedom.

Alfonso unfolded a large yellow kite and they watched it swoop above them. She liked the noise it made, flapping in the wind, and she shook her hair loose to feel the breeze. While the other two went for a stroll, he showed her, laughing, how to fly the kite, holding her hands until she was sure of her strength. When he let go, she lurched forward, jolted by the pull, and they laughed while the other pair, quietly in love, strolled further away, hand in hand.

She had laughed that day and on so many others, but she felt fooled and cheated as soon as she returned to the house. Each morning, she heard Miss Havers collect the post from the door cage, her father's voice in dictation and the typewriter keys pounding.

Every day without respite, Mariquita swept her away to the kitchen, to the dining room, the bedrooms or Frank's room. She swept her to any place rather than allow her to stand still. Only momentarily, suspended to gasp between tasks, Tessa watched Alfonso and Matty follow Joseph to the warehouse, but her sister held her tightly by her new apron strings so that she could not follow.

The garden became her only sanctuary, and she lingered there, where her hands could lie inactive in her lap and she didn't have to hold in her feelings. She would smell the roses, then, after a while, she began to cut a few for her mother's dressing table. Later on, she did the same for Mariquita's and her own, until she also made small displays of flowers for the cook and Abigail and Frank. Out of her sister's jurisdiction, she sewed lavender and rose muslin sachets for all the drawers and slipped scented stems between the sheets in the closet. Her small marks on the house.

Imprisoned by tasks, the days held no moments beyond errands to catch a train or motor bus into town, so she looked forward, more than anything, to the days when Alfonso would take her out, planning all sorts of treats, when she could pretend she was a modern girl living in a modern age and not the repressed daughter of a traditional, old-fashioned father.

After she confessed her thoughts to him, Father Ryan told her to heed her parents and be a dutiful daughter like her sisters.

That same evening, she wrote to Carmen. She told her not to have any dreams for the future about cauliflowers or Brussels sprouts or anything to do with gardens, but to live life for now, because anything later would be an existence. She told her that it was all a lie. They learnt their lessons to no avail, as they might as well stay at home and play in the nursery all day long for the good it did them. As her writing became more erratic, ink smudging under her tears, she muttered about lost dreams and the dissipation of hope and the helplessness of the female condition. When she had finished warning her younger sister of the duplicity of the world, she threw her pen across the room.

"I hate it here!" she shouted.

The next morning, she tore up the letter and watched its ashes catch in the flames of the fire and rise up the chimney. In the afternoon, she posted a little card to Carmen, telling her about the yellow kite and enclosing some pressed sweet peas from the garden because they were the strongest perfumed flowers she could find. If she didn't have the right words, she thought, hopefully, the scent of flowers would jolt the memory of the dreams they'd shared when painting their aspirations under Mariquita's dissatisfied gaze.

ON THE OTHER side of the channel, the young redheaded Corsican, who had learnt his trade amongst the merchants in Marseilles, was now head of a growing perfume empire. He wore the best-cut suits, coloured his hair blonde and was emperor of all he surveyed.

Chapter Eleven

I T WAS AN unexpected day when Mrs. Garcia told Tessa that she would meet her at eleven at the tearoom in Harrods department store, where they would have a cup of coffee and a slice of shortbread.

They travelled together to the centre of town, and while Mrs. Garcia ran errands, Tessa had an hour to herself. There was only one place she wanted to be. She spent the entire hour in Harrods' perfume hall and relished the freedom away from Mariquita's stringent routine. Mrs. Garcia also occasionally broke free, and Tessa wondered if her mother had realised she needed the same. The scents and sights of the perfumes soon cast away any other thought but the beauty of the room, the clink of glass and pop of stoppers.

She imagined François Coty walking by her side, pointing out this and that and leading her to his collection. Later, she'd sit with him, and not her mother, in the tearoom, and he would order a jug of coffee rather than a cup. At the snap of his fingers, the cake trolley would appear, and they would both choose a rich slice of the dark-tasting chocolate torte with its swirls of grated brown and dusting of deepest cocoa powder. She savoured the decadence as the coffee and chocolate merged on her tongue. He had taken off his hat, and they spoke to each other in French, whilst all around chattered in English.

Coty and she spoke freely of deeper matters because no-one else could understand them. He explained how he wished to be her patron and would fund her business in London, selling delicate, English-styled scents, which she cleverly overlaid with the citric of southern Spain and the heady aroma of the deepest chocolate. They would laugh over the names they conjured between them, and his mismatched eyes would gaze only at her.

"May I help you, Miss?"

The words breaking into her reverie were unmistakeably English.

"Thank you," Tessa smiled. "I wondered...may I?"

The assistant lifted a bottle and extracted the stopper, dabbing it lightly onto her wrist. "It's the latest. New this year."

Tessa hadn't seen the name or the shape of the container. She stared at the 'Helena Rubenstein' sign over the assistant's head.

"Thank you," she said, stepping back. Shaking her wrist in an attempt to discard the smell, she imagined Coty's reaction. To her, it smelt unpleasant, but how offensive would it be to him; a scent other than his had stained her skin?

Hurrying to the familiar Coty counter, she frantically dabbed perfume onto her neck and other wrist, behind her ears and onto her handkerchief.

"Madam likes this one?"

Tessa hoped Coty would see her action and pour her another cup of coffee. Carefully, she stepped between the counters, making sure she was not caught out again, but wrapped in his scent alone. It was only then, when she was saturated, that she calmed down. Only then did she look more closely at all the assistants in the vast perfume hall. They did not seem a great deal different from herself. They were young, respectable and did not look as if they would starve to death if they did not dab perfume on ladies' wrists or wrap their purchases with pretty bows. The point was, they did not look as though they needed to work. Surely, she could do the same and her father would not object? She might not be able to learn business from her father, but she could learn a different business and one she had been an apprentice in, since she had made her first perfumes in their small bathroom all those years ago.

She saw herself leaving the house with her brothers after breakfast, catching a train into the heart of the city and disembarking with the masses of young women, all smartly dressed and neatly turned out as they lifted the muslin sheets from the counters and waved their feather dusters over the boxes of perfume and smiled large, professional smiles at the first customers. This she could do. She could belong here.

She hurried back to the Coty stand and leaned across the counter towards a young woman.

"To whom do I speak about acquiring a position?"

The woman stared back, narrow blue eyes and powdered cheeks.

"I beg your pardon, Madam?"

Heat swept across Tessa's face as she realised that a customer could never work at a place she patronised. She smiled and swiftly strode away, past Guerlain, who sneered, past Helena Rubenstein, silenced by shock. She flushed at her ignorance. Her parents would know people who came here, and she saw how inappropriate it would be to dab perfume on her mother's wrist in Harrods' perfume hall when she was not even allowed to do so in the privacy of her mother's bedroom.

IT WAS WEEKS before Tessa escaped again, but she did so this time without her mother, and she went to a place she had never before been. The din in the anonymous typing hall was overwhelming. Even though she had been brought up in the noisiest house in London, she was completely unprepared for it, for this was a very different type of noise. Whereas the barrage in the Garcia household was spontaneous and random, this was regimented like the drum beat of a political march.

She gazed over the rows of young women who sat at desks with their fingers flying over the machines in front of them. The keys moved in a continuous battery of percussion. The manageress of the fourth-floor department handed Tessa a folder.

"As you can see, we're snowed under," she said. "But we can only take you if you're fast. Let's see how you get on."

Tessa saw how she got on. She sat for two hours and came away with her head thumping, her eyes dry and aching and her throat parched. She wanted to immerse herself in a deep bath and soothe away the pain in between her shoulder blades. She knew that working here would not be as easy as she'd thought.

"I see no reason why you shouldn't come back tomorrow," the manageress, whose name had been crowded out of Tessa's head, held out her hand. No, there was no reason except that she did not need to earn a living.

The entire family looked up from their plates when she dragged her feet into the dining room. Mariquita pushed back her chair.

"We were worried—"

"Where have you been?" snapped Mr. Garcia.

His tone took Tessa by surprise.

"I am sorry I am late."

"It is your mother you should be apologising to."

"I'm sorry, Mama."

"Abigail, hand Miss Teresa—"

"Thank you, Abigail, I'm not hungry."

"You will have the courtesy to sit down and eat!" ordered Mr. Garcia.

Tessa sat, and the meal continued for some time in silence, except for the scrape of knife on china plate, before Mr. Garcia said, "Are you going to answer my question?"

"I'm sorry, Papa. I have forgotten what you asked."

"Where have you been that's kept you so late?"

She drooped with fatigue. "I've got a job in a typing pool."

Mariquita's head snapped up. Mrs. Garcia put a whole mushroom in her mouth. Alfonso laughed nervously.

Mr. Garcia glared at him. "Did you put her up to this?"

"No, Papa."

He stared at her. "Who put such a ludicrous idea into your head?"

"No-one." She was far, far too tired. "You don't want me, so I thought I'd see if anyone else did."

"What's the company's name?" asked Joseph, seeing as his father remained speechless with anger.

"Brocklebent Insurance Company," said Tessa.

"Are they in Kensington?" asked Nacho.

"Piccadilly," corrected Tony.

"They're highly respectable," she added. "The other girls look as though they are from good homes."

"She's right, Papa. All sorts work in the city now," added Alfonso.

"No daughter of mine."

"Please, Papa."

"Did you hear me?"

"Yes, Papa, but—"

"Do you understand?"

"Yes, Papa."

Tears sparkled in her eyes, and the lump in her throat, put there by the typing pool, swelled into an overwhelming rock of granite.

"The manageress told me that I was very capable. She thought I was quick and efficient like you always say I am, Papa."

"That was when you were a child! You are a grown woman now and games are over with!"

Her heart raced. Her father continued.

"You are a Garcia. The women in this household do not go into the sordid world of commerce. It is the men who dirty their hands, not the women. The men! Your mother stays at home. Mariquita stays at home. What makes you think you are different? My daughters will all stay at home, cared for by me, until I see fit that they marry. Then, and only then, may they leave this house to take up residence in their husband's home, where they will make absolutely sure that their daughters are brought up in exactly the same manner as they have been raised! Do you hear me? Do I make myself clear?"

He gulped down his food in order to leave the table and his family as quickly as possible, and to find sanctuary behind the door of his study.

Tessa's brothers avoided her eyes and finished every morsel on their plates. Mrs. Garcia was the last to finish eating.

When her father left the room, she did not follow him and nor did anyone else.

Chapter Twelve

Alfonso had suggested they drive down to Farnborough Air Show, but when he broached the subject, Tessa burst into tears, which surprised her even more than it did him.

"I can't believe how much I hate it here," she sobbed by way of explanation, throwing her arms around him. "I couldn't wait to get back, and now all I want to do is to escape."

Escaping from the city, surrounded by crowds surging and unfamiliar contraptions that promised to perform at new heights, Tessa breathed deeply and allowed herself to take in an afternoon's freedom. People massed around them; engines stuttered and thrummed; smells of grass and oil, coffee and fruit mingled. Gradually, she relaxed and began to appreciate the new surroundings and sense of excitement. A flurry of activity caught her attention. Some photographers trailed an important person. Voices were raised. A blonde head. There was wealth there, she decided, then paused. She recognised the figure from a newspaper photograph she'd seen months before.

Luckily, the assembly stood near an aircraft that Alfonso wanted to see. They struggled through the crowd, Tessa keeping her eyes fixed on that blonde head while Alfonso focused on a line of small aircraft. As they got closer, voices grew more distinct, and she made out snatches of conversation.

"He's shorter than I thought."

"But look at the way he's dressed."

"No photographs! I said no cameras!"

An official obscured their view. Alfonso leaned in to Tessa. "I know why you were happy to come," he said. "You do know Mr. Coty dyes his hair, don't you?"

"Everyone knows that, and why not?" She let go of his arm, but she'd lost sight of her hero and spun around, trying to see him again. A shadow fell as a tall, black-haired man in a light suit and straw hat barred her way. She peered around his shoulder. "Excuse me, do you mind?"

Alfonso burst out laughing. "Honestly, sis, let me introduce my good friend, Sandes. What are you doing here? You didn't say you were coming. Tessa! Stop! Sandes, this star-struck female is my sister."

They studied each other for a moment before Tessa twirled around again.

"I am not star-struck. I leave that to my brother. And he is completely fickle. He is in love with *all* the aircraft, not just one."

Both Sandes and Alfonso followed her gaze.

"Rubbish! I'll give you *in love*! Where's he gone?" Alfonso spoke to Sandes. "You've heard of that Coty chap, haven't you? My little sister thinks he's the bee's knees."

"He's the best perfumier in the world and a brilliant businessman. You can't argue with that. That is not love. That is respect."

62

Alfonso raised his hands and guffawed loudly.

"What's wrong with admiring someone who is the greatest in their field?" Tessa protested.

Sandes laughed. "I don't think you can win, Alfonso. It's a pleasure to meet you, Miss Garcia."

"Tessa," corrected Alfonso.

"Tessa. My apologies."

"Oh, don't apologise," said Alfonso. "It's not a day for any of that sort of nonsense."

She held out her hand. "Is Sandes your baptismal name?"

"It's the only one anybody can get out of him," interrupted Alfonso. "My theory is he's got some ghastly name handed down through the generations. That or he's very pompous. Which one is it, Sandes?"

"I like it. It's not something you hear every day." Sandes bowed.

"All right if you two keep each other company while I have a gander at the Wrights' machine?" Alfonso asked. "That's all right with you, isn't it, Tessie?"

She smiled at her eager brother and watched him run off.

"If you want to go as well, Sandes, please don't linger here on my account. I can occupy myself quite easily."

He smiled. "Where would you like to go?"

She looked past his shoulder but couldn't see François Coty or his entourage and pursuing photographers and reporters.

"This is my first time here. I will let you be my guide," she said.

He smiled wider and held out his arm.

As they walked through the crowds, Tessa noticed other women glance at him, so she began to study him more closely, and to notice the material of his suit, the way his hat rested at a slight angle and how thick and dark his eyelashes were against his cheekbones. He looked like he could own a vineyard, or a bank. She couldn't work it out. He smelt fresh and looked elegant, nothing like Alfonso's other friends.

When he steered her across the grass, she decided she didn't mind that he took control.

"We'll get a better view from here," he said.

"We're certainly losing the crowds."

Sandes pointed. "Yes, but look."

Alfonso stood in line next to an airplane at the far side of the field.

"Do you think he's queuing for an autograph?" she asked.

"I think he's hoping for a flight. It's what he came for, isn't it?"

"I should have guessed!" She laughed. "He said he was doing this for me. Are they safe?"

"Well, there's your hero up there right now, so I guess so." A small plane circled above them. "Does it make you want to have a go?"

She shaded her eyes to watch the plane soar. "I'd follow him to Paris, but I'd probably take a boat."

"What would an ordinary fellow have to do to take you for a drive in his motor car?"

She turned her eyes to his. She had never been flirted with before, and she felt awkward and inexperienced.

"Let's go a little further back," Sandes suggested, breaking the silence. "We'll get an even better view. More space for a big smile and a huge wave to Alfonso when it's his turn to be up there in the blue."

She put up her parasol, and they strolled against the crowds.

"You should come with Alfonso to watch England play at Lords," he said. "I have a flat overlooking the grounds. We can have a cocktail every time Hobbs scores an innings."

"I'm afraid I know as little about cricket as I do about flying."

"I'm sure you'll come to many more air shows now that you've had a taster."

"I've only recently returned from school in Belgium, so I feel I have much to catch up on. Convent schools aren't exactly up on the latest fads."

"I'd be glad to be your guide. I know what it's like returning to England after being away. I was at school in Spain with Alfonso. You feel like a fish out of water when you get back, but it doesn't last. You needn't worry. You'll soon feel as though you've never been away."

"It's easier for you boys. You're free to come and go at will."

"Not true at all. I had to stay with my family. You haven't met them!"

"You haven't met mine."

He smiled, though not quite as broadly.

"When Alfonso comes down, we'll drink to our freedom."

"That would be perfect," she said, "but knowing him, he'll charm them so he can stay up all day. We'll be lucky to have him back with us again by sunset."

TESSA COULDN'T RECALL the exact moment she saw the aircraft turn. All the noise around her hushed except for a rushing wind and a high mechanical scream. A burst of flame and then a billow of smoke spiralled down into a silent crumpling of metal. Her ears popped. Only then did she hear the amplified panic and horror of the crowds.

Chapter Thirteen

FROM AN UPSTAIRS window, Tessa watched a man carry a wreath from a van, just as she had watched the delivery of flowers for her mother's vases years before. He trudged up the steps and rang the front doorbell. Abigail's footsteps pealed across the hall. The door opened with its usual rattling letter cage. Voices. The door closed.

She trudged downstairs. The dining room seemed darker than usual. Her father stood by the fireplace and held up a card.

"My sincere condolences," he read. "François Coty. Why on earth would a man we don't know send a wreath to us?"

"Mr. Coty was at Farnborough, Papa," Tessa said. "He must have seen the accident. He likes airplanes like Alfonso does, I mean, did... I suppose it could have been, I, we saw him. I think it's extremely thoughtful."

"There was no need."

"May I see it?"

Mr. Garcia handed her the card and returned to his study without another word. Tessa sat at the table and gazed at the distinctive handwriting. She imagined him sitting at his grand desk and ordering the wreath from the Coty offices in Suresnes or perhaps from his house in the Bois de Boulogne. She pursed her lips, imagining him saying their name and how it would sound with his accent.

Sniffing the card for a trace of scent, she wondered how he would smell if he stood in the room now. Would he smell faintly of a mixture of lemon and musk or perhaps bergamot and sandalwood? She envisaged herself as his assistant, wafting across the room towards him, handing him a letter to sign, him flourishing his pen, formal yet friendly, speaking to her, Tessa Garcia, about something mundane. About lunch. Dinner. Thanking her for the vase of flowers she had placed on his desk that morning. How no-one else made such a gesture. How no-one else took care of his affairs as well as she did.

The telephone on his desk rang. She picked up the receiver.

"The Coty Empire?"

No one spoke on the other end of the line.

The telephone rang again. She stared into the receiver wondering why it kept ringing until she realised the front doorbell to the Garcia house in London was the sound, not a telephone in François Coty's French office. The doorbell rang and rang. Finally, voices.

She replaced the imaginary receiver on the imaginary cradle.

Voices in the hallway became clear.

"I wish to offer my condolences," a man said.

Footsteps faded away. Two pairs of footsteps came back.

"I wish to offer you my condolences, sir."

She clasped her hands, looking out of the window. The door from the hall opened. Her father stooped into the room, followed by the tall figure of Sandes. Mr. Garcia paused by the fireplace, and she joined him, her arm touching his sleeve.

She hadn't seen Sandes since the accident and the drive home that she didn't remember. She'd hurt him, she knew that, by struggling as he had carried her away from the burning wreckage. She must have hurt him because she had twisted and kicked, struck with her elbows and fists.

"Is there anything I can do for you?" His eyes flickered in her direction before he looked at Mr. Garcia.

"Thank you. We are all...as you can see."

She looked at her father, realising again that he didn't know what to do and that he had shrunk, in more ways than it showed on the outside.

"Thank you for calling," she said. "You are kind."

SEVERAL DAYS LATER, that same room filled with sombre figures. The large table had been pushed to one end, leaving a chasm of space and abandoned chairs. Abigail moved between the mourners offering rich fruitcake and glasses of sherry. Several people sat at the table, eating meat and salad. Mrs. Garcia sat with them, sipping coffee with a spoonful of brandy for warmth. She talked vivaciously, though her eyes were shadowed through lack of sleep. Mariquita strode from group to group, asking if they needed more cake. On a window seat, half-hidden by a curtain, Nacho and Matty sat either side of a distraught Carmen. Joseph circulated like a businessman and Tony swapped news with associates he had not seen for weeks as if they were at a work's party. Frank remained upstairs. He didn't like the smell of cigarettes. They hurt his lungs. On the adjacent window seat to her siblings, Tessa sat beside Sandes. They stared out at the freshly cut grass and commented on the garden sagging under the weight of the season.

"Would it help if I took you out to tea sometime?" he asked.

"I think we have all we need here."

"No, I meant, not today, another day. Later on, when you are wanting to go out. I could tell, that you liked—"

"I don't think I could leave the house for quite a while."

"Please forgive me. I only thought that it would be a distraction, and I know I would enjoy your company."

"Thank you, but I do not need distracting, and as for company, I think you would find better elsewhere. I'm sure you understand."

The clatter of china, cups against saucers, teaspoons, hushed voices, a louder word, a cough, a laugh, all sounds crammed in one room and she struggled not to panic. Her heart pounded too fast. There were too many people and not enough air, and Sandes sat so close she felt the heat of his skin.

"My apologies. I didn't mean to offend you." He stood and bowed. His brown eyes looked hurt, like a puppy's.

"You didn't..."

But already, the slow-moving figures engulfed him. She stared at the garden again, wishing they hadn't gone to the air show and that Alfonso would appear.

The mellow sun made the fluttering leaves glow. Alfonso would have liked to see them. They'd have kicked up the heaps, scattering browns, russets and golds to the wind. Laughter. The gardener telling them off. Hearing Joseph's voice, she turned to see why he spoke so loudly. He was shaking hands with Sandes. She'd not noticed before how thin Joseph seemed in comparison to the larger man. Sandes' hands seemed huge and strong, grasping Joseph's delicate fingers. Tessa rose and walked towards them, but Mariquita intercepted.

"I feel we should stop serving the sherry now, then they will all go. Don't you agree?"

"I don't know. You'd better ask Papa."

"I don't want to bother him. Come and see how much is left."

Mariquita led the way to the sideboard on which stood decanters, bottles, glasses and plates scattered with fruitcake crumbs. Abigail filled small glasses with sherry and placed them on a tray. The liquid sparkled amber in the lamplight and smelt of warm acorns and moist earth.

"People are still drinking," she said. "They seem to want to stay, and they're talking about Alfonso and how much they thought of him…"

Mariquita frowned as Tessa wove through the guests. In the hallway, Joseph opened the front door, letting in the breeze from the street.

"It's all right, Joseph, I'll see Mr. Sandes out."

Joseph nodded and walked past his sister and Alfonso's friend, back into the dining room. Sandes pulled on his gloves while Tessa picked up the hat that rested on the hall table.

She gripped the hat tighter. "It was good of you to come. You didn't have to."

"Your parents seem to be bearing up very well," he said.

"We will all miss Alfonso, you know. He was my best friend as well as my brother. I would like to go out to tea soon," she said, handing him his hat.

TWO WEEKS LATER, Tessa looked at her hands resting in her lap, trying to work out if she felt guilt or relief at leaving the house. Everyone else in the tearoom seemed to behave as if tragedy had never touched them. It seemed incredulous that they carried on as if nothing bad ever happened. It was as though she carried a secret and she wanted to shout at them to stop laughing, stop chattering, to stop being happy.

The waitress placed buttered teacakes on the table next to the teapot. Tessa could tell from the way Sandes muttered, "Thank you," that he was smiling. Even his pleasure felt wrong, and he didn't seem to realise how out of place it was.

"We should do this every week," he said.

Tears trickled down her cheeks, and she fumbled in her bag. A piece of white cotton caught her eye. He held out his handkerchief. Taking it, she hid herself inside.

"Would you like me to take you home?" he asked. "This is too soon, isn't it?"

"No! I mean, no. Thank you. I am fine. I'll be fine."

She'd said *fine*. That word hid worlds. It shut people up, and maybe that was why it became a refrain.

He refilled her cup and they sat in silence, surrounded by incessant voices. She didn't know what to say. He didn't know what to say. This was a mistake. They did not know each other. She could never talk to him like she talked to Alfonso; she'd never talk to anyone like she'd talked to her brother. She dabbed her eyes and held herself in.

"I should have let you invite *me* to tea when you were ready," he said.

She smiled, raising a further fountain of tears. To stop him looking at her, she held out his handkerchief, and he took it, pushing it into his pocket.

"Toasted teacakes are my favourite," she said. She bit into the toast so that butter oozed over her fingers.

"You are pleased to be out of the house, aren't you?"

She glanced around the room. "You don't know our house. This is a morgue compared to home."

As soon as she saw the expression on his face, she knew she'd said the wrong thing. It was hard to believe that she'd mentioned the word morgue when she'd been so distraught a moment earlier. She dabbed her mouth. He would not think of her as a devout convent girl in mourning for her brother when she said things like that.

"I'll take you somewhere that's like neither, after we've finished," he said. "Somewhere to find peace."

LATER, THEY STOOD side by side in the National Art Gallery, staring at a painting by Matisse. The hush of fellow visitors' footsteps and whispers brushed past them like feathers. The blue of the paintings lulled; purple calmed. She brushed Sandes' arm, and the haze of tranquillity encircled her. Here she could sleep. Here, the pain lost its edges. Her bones curled and she tipped sideways.

Darkness enveloped her before she hit the ground, and she felt nothing of her limbs striking the wooden boards. It could have been hours, minutes or seconds before she opened her eyes. A blurred face stared down at her. Brown eyes. A halo of black hair. Features came into focus. A voice.

"Hello," it said. "Welcome back."

Chapter Fourteen

A FEEBLE SUN LIGHTENED the grey November sky. The clock struck three, and Tessa turned on the lamps. A fire blazed in the grate, making the polished wood of the furniture gleam. Mr. Garcia rummaged through the burning coals with a poker until Mrs. Garcia snapped that he would put it out. Mariquita sat next to her mother and poured tea from a large silver teapot. She added a splash of milk to a cup and handed it to her father, who took it, looked down at the poker, then back at the cup. Tessa prised a small sugar daisy from a cake atop the stand on the sideboard.

"Happy Birthday," said Sandes, holding out a lilac-wrapped box.

"Open it over here, so that we can all see," beckoned her sister.

Tessa sat down, and everyone watched her pull the end of purple ribbon so that the bows slid out and the paper loosened. Mariquita took the ribbon from her and wound it into a roll. Mrs. Garcia straightened her skirt. Joseph glanced at his watch, ignoring Tony and Nacho, who filled their plates with muffins and sandwiches. Only Matty leant over the back of her chair, his chin almost resting on her shoulder in order to see. Frank looked away, into the burning centre of the fire, seeing images that the others could not. Sandes remained standing by the sideboard.

"Thank you." She held up a bracelet. "It's beautiful."

Garnets sparkled in the light. Crossing quickly, Sandes took it from her and fastened it around her wrist, the oval links resting lightly on her skin. She watched his fingers deftly pulling back the catch, inserting the loop and releasing the hold.

"Well done," said Matty.

Mrs. Garcia nodded. Mariquita lifted the poker from her father's hand. The boys all agreed, *yes, it's beautiful*, without looking. Matty slapped Sandes on the back. Frank glanced back at them over his shoulder and held up his thumb.

"It's lovely." She turned her wrist, pleased with the contrast between the deep red and her skin.

"I'm glad you like it," said Sandes as he accepted a cup from Mrs. Garcia. "I wasn't positive you would."

"Tessa doesn't have anything like it."

"It's a shame Carmen went back," said Mariquita. "She loves cake."

"Carmen's place is at school," their mother snapped. "She was right to want to go back."

Later, when they had sung 'Happy Birthday' and the cake had been sliced and eaten, Mr. Garcia sat behind a newspaper while Joseph tried to engage him in conversation. Tony, Nacho and Matty made a hasty exit, and Mariquita took up her crochet work. Tessa wished that the day was over; it was Alfonso she missed, not Carmen. Everyone tried to make up for it, but it wasn't the same without him. She wished Sandes would leave so she could look over the pile of presents, quietly go down to the kitchen to show her bracelet, eat a second slice of cake perhaps, savour the sugared flowers melting in her mouth and think the thoughts she wanted to think about. Sandes seemed reluctant to leave even though the darkness outside suggested it was later than the time on the clock. The bracelet twisted cold against her skin.

"Who wants to play cards?" she asked.

"I will," Sandes answered quickly, crossing to the table and pulling out a chair.

Shaking her head, Mariquita held up the crocheted mat; Mrs. Garcia did not even look up from her book. Tessa picked out a deck of cards from the bureau and waved them above her head.

"Anyone else?"

"You two play," said Joseph before he realised Mr. Garcia quietly snored behind the newspaper.

Tessa sat down. "What do you want to play?" she asked.

"What can we play with two?"

Every word he said sounded loaded with meaning.

"Pontoon? We don't have to think too hard at that and it doesn't go on all night."

THE NEXT SUNDAY, after they had knelt side by side and accepted the body and the blood of Christ, they had returned to their seats, extremely aware of the other's body and pulse, and Sandes was once again a visitor in the Garcia house. On this afternoon, the grey sky threatened, but it didn't prevent her from showing him the garden. She didn't trust the heat of the fire or another game of cards when their hands constantly touched and his breath made her already warm cheeks warmer. They couldn't help but notice, on their progress past the bewildered flowerbeds, Mariquita keeping an eye from the long windows of the house.

"She's very protective," said Sandes, standing aside to let Tessa walk down the narrow path in front of him.

"She thinks that's why she's been put on this Earth, to make sure we know right from wrong."

"And do you?"

Tessa laughed for the first time. "It's all down to perspective."

At the end of the path, a gate led into another section of the garden. He leaned past Tessa and lifted the latch.

"Do you want to go on?" She turned suddenly, aware that they would no longer be in sight of the house and that she would be entirely alone with him. Escaping the heat of the drawing room began to sound a ludicrous hope.

"Of course." He held the gate for her to pass through. It closed behind them with a snap and they entered the wild section of the garden where the trees had already given up their apples and the last remaining roses made a gasp of brown-tinged colour.

"Smell this one, though it may have lost its scent by now," she suggested, lifting her hand to cup a salmon-pink blossom.

She was aware he studied her as he followed behind. She felt his eyes like hands on the small of her back, and she turned for him to join her so that in the open space they could walk side by side. All too soon, they passed through an archway to be met by Mariquita's watchful face in the distant window. Tessa glanced up at the darkening clouds and shivered.

"Let me show you Joseph's attempts at topiary," she said.

Their footsteps crunched on the gravel until heavy rain drops fell with increasing speed and a rumble of thunder made them halt.

He pointed. "Can we shelter there?"

Already soaked, they ran to the summerhouse. Tessa flung open the French windows, and they stumbled inside. Mist shrouded the shapes of box and evergreen and the sky grew darker, while inside it smelt dull and musty now that summer was over.

Shivering again, she noticed a few candles lying on a wicker table. "Have you any matches?"

He reached into his pocket, extracted a small box and struck one. As the smell of sulphur dissipated, the candles burned, illuminating folded deckchairs, wicker tables and large parasols.

"We were lucky," Sandes said, stepping towards the doors to watch the rain bounce off the path.

Tessa moved to stand beside him. A flash of lightning illuminated the sky. Thunder galloped close by.

"Do you think your sister will dash down here and march us back to the house?"

"She'll know we've found shelter, so I wouldn't be surprised."

Her hair clung to her scalp and curls of damp trailed down her dress. She wiped her cheeks with the sleeve of her long cardigan.

"So? How long before you think she will be joining us?"

"Stop it." She squeezed the ends of her hair, making it drip. "Of course she won't."

"Then we'll have to stay here until the storm subsides."

She couldn't tell if he was joking or serious.

"Well, I don't want to be struck by a lightning bolt," she said.

"So, it's only the two of us, and we've no cards to keep us occupied." He looked around the summerhouse that the candles barely illuminated. "I think we'll have to make ourselves more comfortable," he said. "Are there any more candles?"

"I will look." She moved towards an old table and pulled out a drawer.

"It doesn't matter. Come and sit here, and we can keep watch for invaders."

He pulled two Lloyd Loom chairs to the entrance. Holding up a blanket, he tucked it around her. And then, without warning, he fell on his knees and rested his head in her lap. Without saying a word, she looked down at his dark head and broad shoulders. She could feel the weight of his skull on her thighs and his hands resting where they had tucked in the rug. Slowly, she raised her hand and placed it on his hair. The only sound was that of the rain battering the wooden roof and striking the path. His warm breath penetrated through the blanket.

After a while, he raised a tear-stained face.

"Oh Sandes, what's the matter?"

"I'm sorry," he said, pushing against the arms of the chair to stand. "I don't know what came over me."

He wiped his face and turned his back on her.

"It's hard not to think about Alfonso," she said.

She wanted to put her arms around him and tell him that she cried every day, but she didn't because a different emotion rose within her. The need to comfort him seemed so strange, she pushed it away. Rain bent the leaves, dripping onto the grass, saturating the earth, thudding on the roof, bouncing on the path. The day seemed to bond together, the thunder, dripping trees and the never-ending tears. She stood by him in the doorway and touched his hand. His eyes once again filled with tears and he wrapped his arms around her. It seemed natural to hug him back.

MARIQUITA WATCHED RIVULETS teem down the windowpane. She was angry that she had let them go out into the garden when it was so obviously going to pour down. She knew that they would find shelter in the summerhouse. She would have preferred to see them appearing out of the mist with the rain drenching their clothes and with her immediately dispatching Sandes. She was angry that she was not right now running a steaming bath with floral smelling salts and helping her sister peel off her wet garments down to her saturated and now transparent underclothes, which she would allow, just this once, to be dropped onto the bathroom floor.

She wiped the window and tried to make out if they had indeed sheltered in the summerhouse or whether they were running towards her. The mist had settled in, and with it the dark. She hated the thought of Sandes drying her sister's face and of them standing together, damp and breathless from their dash through the rain. She wanted to go and grasp Tessa's hand and drag her over the grass, not caring that they were soaked. They would leave him standing alone. He could stay and watch them go, as he weathered out the storm, or run for the gate and his car or a cab, or whatever. She didn't care. All she cared about was that she and Tessa dried themselves in the privacy of their bedroom. With a decisive stride, she snapped down the bolts of the French windows and opened them wide. Taking a deep breath and pulling her shawl over her head, she marched across the patio.

Chapter Fifteen

MARIQUITA WOULD HAVE gone with Tessa to change the flowers on Alfonso's grave if Sandes hadn't asked to accompany them. Instead, making sure they understood her displeasure, and holding the fact that she'd been the one who'd warmed her sister with a hot bath and dry clothes, she took herself down to the church with a bunch of carnations that she rammed into vases while hurling insults at alabaster Mary.

In the cemetery, Sandes paced up and down on the paved path whilst Tessa arranged purple irises into the container on the family grave.

"Mariquita doesn't like you," she said.

"Does that bother you?"

"Does it bother you?"

He crouched beside her.

"I'm not keen on irises, but Alfonso liked them," she said.

"What do you like?"

"Any flower that has a scent."

"Roses?"

She nodded and, brushing herself down, strolled towards the trees. Sandes tapped Alfonso's gravestone, then jogged after her.

"Your sister will end up liking me," he said. "Everyone does."

He beat the air with his hat, and Tessa glanced at his profile. All she'd learned at the convent seemed unimportant and useless. Sandes didn't speak French. Miss Havers still didn't leave. Now, she strolled around art galleries as he told her about Chimera and about a painter called Picasso who was shocking the world. When they walked across Regent's Park, she imagined which artists they would talk about in fifty years' time or if they'd be too busy with the million things Mariquita said a married woman had to do, to have anything at all to say to each other.

But he did make her forget the anger that her father's secretary made her feel. When she was with Sandes, it didn't seem to matter that she would never again take her father's post and sit opposite him at his desk, reading out his correspondence, typing letters and finding new customers. Building an empire.

When she was with Sandes, she felt as though nothing like that mattered. She smiled until her cheeks ached because now she could tease him as she had teased and been teased by Alfonso.

"What are you thinking?" he asked.

"The fact that irises don't smell."

"Nonsense. You're always thinking or planning."

"I'm thinking that I like Matisse more than Picasso. And I love Mr. Kandinsky's brightness and the energy in his paintings."

He glanced at a newspaper stand announcing that Prince Albert was set to wed Lady Elizabeth Bowes-Lyon.

"What are *you* thinking about?" she mocked. "You're always thinking and planning…"

"That you are a breath of fresh air."

No-one had ever said anything like that to her or looked at her with the expression Sandes held on his face. *A breath of fresh air.* What did that mean but new beginnings, spring, rebirth and freedom?

Wandering through the park, they meandered past the boating ponds and watched courting couples sneak a moment's solitude in the white rowing boats. They sauntered past the pavilions, where passion tea and flirtation sandwiches were being served.

SANDES WALKED LIKE a long-married man with a bevy of children around him, whilst Tessa still glowed like a woman on the brink. They meandered under the shade of the evergreens where the light turned opaque and the air dulled all outside noise. The grass was soft with sandy pine needles. It was here that he first attempted to kiss her and where she let him. Her neck felt only slightly uncomfortable as she stretched to meet his lips. It was a brief kiss, caught between a pine and an ancient oak, but the unfamiliarity of it made her desire to sample more. Sandes found her willingness at odds with his idea of decorum but was glad that her lips had moved against his and not remained rigid as he had found other lips do.

That evening, when Mr. and Mrs. Garcia said goodnight, with promises extracted that he would be brief in his farewell, he knew he was accepted. The firelight crackled. Tessa stood by the door of the room, her hand on the handle. He looked back regretfully at the softness of the velvet sofa and warm firelight. The hall seemed cold and uncharitable. She followed his gaze and smiled as if she knew. It was again brief, but the kiss made him aware that soon he would be making a proposal. He was not to know that within twenty-four hours, his plans would be thrown into turmoil.

Chapter Sixteen

A T THE TOP of the stairs, Tessa stood, holding a pile of freshly folded pillowcases and watching Miss Havers open the front door to take letters from the postman. Miss Havers glanced up as she returned down the hall to the study, but neither said a word and the study door closed.

After a moment, Tessa placed the pillowcases on the second shelf of the linen closet, next to lavender-scented sheets. She breathed in deeply, trying to calm her thoughts.

"Tessa?" Mariquita's voice shattered her reverie and she followed its call to where Frank sat, a plaid rug around his shoulders, in the armchair by his bedroom window.

"Read to him for a while," Mariquita said, holding out a book.

"D'you want me to, Frank?"

He didn't answer but continued to stare through the glass.

"Of course he does. Don't you, Frank?" No answer. "He doesn't know what he wants," Mariquita said. Her feet fell heavily on the floor as she left the room.

Tessa looked down at the book cover. "*War and Peace.* Is this what you're reading?" She studied the bookshelf and replaced the heavy tome, taking down a copy of

The Story of Peter Pan instead. She held it up. "It's ages since I read this."

Frank coughed.

"Do you want me to fetch you some water?"

He turned his head towards the full glass on the table next to his chair.

She sat and opened the book. "Part one. Early days." She glanced up at Frank. He had closed his eyes. He'd always listened to stories the same way. She continued.

"In one of the nicest nurseries in the world, there were beds for three young people called John Napoleon, Wendy Moira Angela, and Michael, the children of Mr. and Mrs. Darling..."

Gradually, Frank's rough breathing changed with the heaviness of sleep, but Tessa kept reading because she found the world of Never-Never-Never Land preferable to that of the Garcia *Forever-Ever-Ever*.

In the background, Mariquita's voice rang out, letting everyone know that she was laying the dining table for lunch. Abigail could be heard beating the bedroom rugs. The harsh banging of the typewriter keys and the rolling pin flattening pastry on the kitchen table added to the household noise.

Although she couldn't hear Mrs. Garcia, Tessa sensed her unhappiness as though it were drumming through the walls, and she paused to hear if anyone else in the house had noticed. Feeling easier, she let the words on the page blur and tried to picture reading *Peter* to her own children in a white nursery, filled with toys and paintings. She frowned. She couldn't imagine kissing soft cheeks goodnight or stepping aside to allow Sandes to do the same. She couldn't see him, only her father's face, bending to kiss her goodnight as she lay, ready for sleep in her own bed.

"Read me the last chapter," Frank said. His eyes remained closed.

She flicked through the pages.

"The only difficulty lay with Peter. Much as at first sight he loved Mrs. Darling, much as he loved Wendy, he couldn't consent to grow up…"

She continued to read, and Frank breathed more quietly. She knew that he was dreaming that every word spoken aloud made the world she read about real.

"So at last it was arranged that he fly back alone to the Never-Never-Never Land," Frank continued for her as if in a trance. "High in the treetops of the Never-Never-Never Land, Tinker Bell placed the little house that was built for Wendy."

They sat and listened to the typewriter and the heavy cutlery making contact with the spotless tablecloth.

"I should call you Peter Pan."

Frank smiled. "Yes, please. I'd like that."

Tessa looked at her brother who had been damaged irreparably by the gas at Ypres.

"But I don't want to be Wendy," she said.

IT HAD NOT taken long for Tessa to decide that she would never marry. She felt it as a gentle lifting of blinds. Sandes felt it as the dropping of a sash window, and he fought hard to make it re-open. However, it was Mariquita's reaction that shocked Tessa most.

She flung the roses on the table. For her, this was the culmination of Tessa's inexcusable behaviour. Tessa had refused to see him, talk to him, even have tea with him. Now she refused his flowers. She had left the room when he had been admitted to the house, leaving Mariquita to make pleasantries about the roses.

Mariquita could tell that Sandes hardly noticed her, not because he was in love with Tessa, but because Tessa was lovely and she was not. She hated him more than ever.

"You cannot treat him like this!" she shouted.

"He is a friend, not my fiancé."

"He could be, if you'd let him."

"I don't see what all the fuss is about. He hasn't mentioned marriage. It is Alfonso we have in common, that is all."

"You're blind! He is in love with you!"

"I suppose we have airplanes in common too."

"I'm going to ask him."

Tessa caught her sister's arm. "You are not."

Mariquita easily shook free, and they glared at each other.

"It's my life," said Tessa.

"You're part of a family. It is a family decision."

They didn't hear Mrs. Garcia enter the room.

"He is too good for either of you," she said.

SEVERAL DAYS AFTER Tessa had first refused to take afternoon tea with him, Sandes stood at a loss by the Coty perfume counter in Harrods. The sales assistant was only too pleased to assist him, but he dashed off before she was able to demonstrate her charms.

Aware of him watching her from behind the Guerlain display, Tessa advanced on the counter and picked up a bottle. No sooner had she opened it than he marched to her side.

"May I?" He lifted the bottle from her hand and smelt its aroma.

The pretty assistant beamed. "La Feuillaison is a perfect choice for Madam, but if I may suggest, it is best smelt on the actual skin."

Sandes dabbed a little on his wrist and inhaled, meeting Tessa's gaze. "Would you like to try it?"

If she had been Peter Pan, she would have stamped her feet and flown at dangerous speed, skimming that ceiling.

"I hope that's not for me," she said.

The assistant looked at them both. He laughed.

"Not want a bottle of perfume? That's not like you."

"I have it already."

Tension shimmered between them.

"Did you like the roses?" he asked once the assistant had returned the bottle to the display.

"Yes, they are beautiful."

"Mariquita told me you were ill. You are feeling better?"

"I am, thank you. I thought some fresh air would do me good. I wouldn't have thought this was a place you frequented." She turned to walk away.

"Tessa?"

She nodded goodbye. "I have a sore throat. I shouldn't have come."

"Then let me take you to tea," he said, catching up. "A hot drink will be what you need."

"I can't. I must go home. Goodbye."

Sandes followed her across the perfume hall, past Guerlain and Helena Rubenstein.

"What's wrong?" he asked. "What have I done?"

"I can't breathe."

He took her arm and led her outside, but she pulled herself free.

"Tell me what is wrong," he insisted.

"Please, let me go."

"Is something troubling you?"

"Mariquita needs me. You see, Mama's in her room and..."

An angry cloud passed over his face. "I understand."

"No, you don't," She couldn't stop herself. "I feel trapped. And I haven't done anything with my life. I haven't...and I've so much I want to do.

"And you must. I wouldn't stop you."

"I like you very much. You're Alfonso's friend."

"I'm your friend too, and I hope more than that, dear Tessa."

She shook her head. "It's too soon. It's a mistake—can't we be friends? Like you and Alfonso?"

He touched his hat. "My apologies. Another time, perhaps, when you're feeling more yourself," he said, before disappearing into the crowd.

Chapter Seventeen

"WHY IS IT, as soon as you say something aloud, it's no longer what you mean?"

Tessa looked at Alfonso's name carved clean in the stone. Mariquita unwrapped a bunch of tulips.

"Maybe it's other people that don't listen properly," she said. "Their definition of words isn't the same as yours."

Tessa stared at Alfonso's dates. *1900 – 1920.* He would never worry about being misunderstood. She wondered if all men were untroubled about their thoughts being translated intact. Joseph was confident that his orders were understood, though she was less sure of her father. He seemed to speak less and less nowadays. Maybe he had some inkling.

She looked around at the bright-yellow bank of daffodils that bordered the cemetery. "Do you think Father Ryan understands Carmen?"

"No-one understands what's going on in that girl's head."

Carmen didn't seem to care if she was understood or not.

Mariquita passed the tight-budded flowers. "You arrange them."

Tessa had picked them from the garden barely an hour ago. The days passed so slowly, yet the months had flown by since she'd last seen Sandes.

"I feel as if life is over," she said, holding out her hand for more stems.

A passer-by would smile sentimentally at the sight of the two dark sisters sombrely tending their brother's grave.

Others visiting their loved ones would be satisfied that the flowers on the grave were changed before they had time to droop. Tessa wasn't satisfied. She was bored. Mariquita, on the other hand, seemed resigned to being satisfied with her place in life.

"Do you think I've been cruel?" Tessa asked, breaking one of the stems.

"About what?"

"I think I have."

"If you're still going on about Sandes, then no, you weren't cruel. You were honest."

"I didn't do it very well."

"You did it."

"Yes," confirmed Tessa. "I did it."

"All that matters is that you are sure you don't want Sandes as a husband. Are you sure?"

"I don't want any type of husband."

"I've no experience of that, and I doubt I ever will, but you should be grateful anyone wants you at all."

"Why should I be grateful? What about him being grateful?"

"He can ask someone else. You have to wait to be asked. That's why you should be grateful. Some people don't have that luxury."

"Why can't a woman ask a man? There'd be none of this hanging around."

"Now you're being stupid."

Both fell silent, aware that no-one would ask Mariquita for her hand in marriage but each too respectful of the other to argue otherwise.

"I miss Alfonso," said Tessa.

"I wish Mama would visit him."

"She does."

"She never leaves any flowers," Mariquita said, crumpling the paper in her fists.

"I think she just sits."

"Have you been with her?"

Tessa shot her sister a glance that told her all she needed to know.

"Do you think Papa's all right?" she asked as they strolled back towards the gates.

Mariquita shrugged. He could look after himself.

AT FIVE O'CLOCK, once Miss Havers had left the house, Tessa carefully carried a cup of tea across the hall and tapped on the study door.

"Come in."

Mr. Garcia sat behind his desk. She carried his tea to him and sat opposite, watching as he sipped.

"Busy day?" she asked.

Mr. Garcia popped a Liquorice Allsort into his mouth before holding out the bag.

"I haven't done anything to deserve one," she said.

"Take one anyway."

She took a black-and-white sweet and tasted the comfort of it in her mouth.

"You've never asked why Sandes won't be calling anymore," she mumbled, her cheek bulging.

Mr. Garcia looked at his daughter. "Poor chap. Does he really not suit?"

"You're pleased, though?"

"Any fool can get married."

"You're married."

Mr. Garcia smiled. "I wasn't a young shaver when I married your mother."

"Sandes is quite old."

"Not so old, my dear."

"How did you know Mama was the right one for you? Was it love at first sight?"

"Love isn't always the best motive for getting married, Tessa. There are other reasons."

"I don't love him," she said.

"Ah yes, but you liked him a little?"

"A little."

They sucked on the strange combination of rough and smooth and smiled at each other. She relaxed in her chair. This was like old times, and he was behaving like the father she knew.

"Why don't you get rid of Miss Havers?" she asked.

The contented expression disappeared from his face. "What's happened?"

She pulled herself up straight. "Nothing. I thought, as I've nothing to do and Mariquita doesn't need me—

you know she runs the house like an army officer..."
She paused. "May I be your secretary again?"

"I have no reason to let Miss Havers go."

"Aren't I enough reason? I can do everything she does."

"Tessa, I told you, Miss Havers needs to work.
You do not."

"I'm not meaning for money. I don't want that, merely
the occasional Allsort. It's for my mind. I'm going mad.
Please, Papa, let me deal with your correspondence again.
I can deal with your letters to the bank—I know there are
loads. I can look for new places to send our sherry and...
Miss Havers will easily get another job. The city is crying
out for people."

"No!" Mr. Garcia raised his voice. "I cannot allow any
of my daughters to do that."

"Mariquita doesn't want to and Carmen certainly
won't be interested, but I want to. Don't you remember
how helpful I was?"

Mr. Garcia did not answer for some time. Eventually,
he said, "I think it's time you ran along. I have some things
I want to finish."

"May I help you? Tell me what to do. I can do anything."

MR. GARCIA SIGHED. He wanted to go to bed but knew
he would not sleep. He wanted to climb on a boat heading
for Spain and arrive feeling the warmth of the sun and
the security of his childhood home.

"No, I can manage. Besides, aren't you going out with
Sandes this evening?"

"Papa! Weren't you listening? I told you. I shan't be seeing him anymore."

"Won't you? Oh. Poor chap. Well, be off with you. Close the door, there's a good girl."

TESSA STOOD UP slowly. "Papa?"

He looked up at her with his dark, soft eyes. She could never be angry with him. He looked like a sad two-year-old with an ancient face, and it made Tessa feel like the parent and him the child.

Chapter Eighteen

A BREEZE ALMOST BLEW off her hat as she strolled towards Harrods for the second time that week. While fixing it more firmly, she looked at the display of L'Eau de Coty in the window. The display fronted the perfume department, and Tessa, too late, realised she shouldn't have come. It was supposed to cheer her, but it rubbed like salt in a wound. A world she couldn't enter. Only one place of work had accepted her, and although her father would rant and rave, maybe she could go back to that office full of typewriters and drown herself in sound. She'd hate it, but better that than the numbness of their house.

Shapes moved temptingly behind the large windows. It was too much, but as she turned away, a familiar figure caught her eye. She recognised Sandes instantly and felt a rush of blood to her temples. He studied a container that an assistant held out for him. She strained to see which Coty perfume it could be, wondering if he were buying it for her in the hope that such a gift would bring her back to him now that spring and hope were in the air.

INSIDE HARRODS' PERFUME hall, Sandes strolled to another counter and wondered if his mother would like the scent he picked up. She always seemed to smell of the same one, ever since he'd been a boy. His father certainly wouldn't think of buying it for her. Tessa had taught him the power of the right aroma on the right woman's skin, and he wanted his mother to have that. It would be gratifying to place it by her napkin at the dining table on her birthday when they sat down in the evening to celebrate. He imagined watching her pull the silk ribbon and ask, with an intrigued smile, what it was so that he would be called upon to explain it was the latest perfume by someone called Guerlain. He felt that Guerlain would suit his mother. It sounded discreet, unflashy, unlike all he knew of François Coty.

He held out the bottle. "What do you think, Elizabeth?"

He'd known Elizabeth Browne for years. Their families got on. She, too, looked discreet and unflashy. She was tall and sinewy, with fine, shining fair hair and deep-set blue eyes. Elegant. Calm.

She curled her long fingers around the bottle. "This one?" She dabbed the barest amount on her wrist. Holding out her slender arm, she nodded for Sandes to smell the skin where thin strands of blue vein neared the surface.

"She'll like that," he confirmed and handed the bottle to the assistant. "Now you must choose something for helping."

Elizabeth pretended surprise. "Oh, no, it was my pleasure."

"I insist."

She swept her eyes over the counter. "I love them all."

"If you want to look elsewhere?"

"No, Guerlain is my favourite. I'm trying to make up my mind, and I don't want to get the same as your mother!"

"Of course, you most certainly don't want the same!"

"Perhaps a powder?"

"Someone told me that Coty makes them."

"I'm quite happy with the choice here." She smiled. "Thank you."

He looked at the assortment of bottles, relieved he wouldn't have to go back to the Coty counter and be reminded of Tessa even more than being so close to perfume already made him feel.

OUTSIDE, TESSA TURNED from the window, telling herself that she was pleased he had replaced both her and Coty.

AS THE SKY darkened and the first heavy drops of rain began to fall, reluctant to return home defeated, Tessa entered the Garcia Warehouse for Wines and Fine Sherry in a much seedier part of the city. She was wondering if everyone had gone home when Joseph strolled down one of the aisles bordered by pale wooden crates bearing the Garcia name.

"You have to give me something to do," she announced, hurrying towards him.

"What are you doing here? Has something happened at home?"

He sounded exactly like her father, and she slapped her palm over the Garcia name on the nearest crate.

"I want something to do! I'll explode if you don't give me something to do."

"Well, don't explode here." Joseph strolled back the way he had come.

Tessa caught him up. "I'm serious, Joseph. You know I can type. I'm good at figures. I'll work hard, you know I will."

He turned with the same exasperation as their mother when they followed her along the street or around the house.

"Is Papa with you?" he asked.

"No, he's at home."

"You shouldn't be here on your own."

"It's not as if this is some strange office building. It belongs to us."

"It's not a suitable place for you. Come with me and I'll find someone to take you home."

"Joseph! I am perfectly capable. I just...I need to do something. I need to work."

"As I suggested, I'll have you taken home."

"Mariquita and I are as capable as Tony and Nacho, but oh no, we've got to stay cooped up in the house, being stifled alive like two decrepit chickens."

JOSEPH STARED AT her in disbelief. He only knew what he felt he needed to know about his younger brothers and sisters, particularly the sisters. Mariquita ran the house, Carmen was at the convent, and Tessa was a flighty young woman who was in love with Alfonso's chum, Sandes... or was it Coty somebody?

102

"Have you and Mariquita fallen out again?"

"I haven't fallen out with anyone."

"Then why aren't you at home?"

"I want you to give me a job. I'm serious. I want to work here with you."

"Did Papa send you down?"

"Yes. No. You're in charge of the warehouse. It's up to you."

"I cannot go behind his back."

"He won't mind."

"Of course he'll mind. It's his business and you're his daughter."

"Exactly. We're a family business. We're meant to run it together."

"You are impossible. You're going home."

"Papa's distracted. He doesn't need to know," Tessa persisted.

"Did that fellow Coty put you up to this?"

"What?"

"Sandes, then?"

"It's nothing to do with anyone else. Papa has outdated ideas, that's all. Since the war, plenty of women work."

"Stop. Stop now. You've said enough."

"What about the office?"

"I will not find you a position here!"

"For goodness' sake, Joseph, other businesses employ women. You're as old-fashioned as Papa. Even Mr. Coty's wife works."

"I knew I'd heard of him. It's that perfume maker, isn't it? I knew you'd got this idea from somewhere.

Papa must be sick of hearing that man's name. This is not a perfume business. This is the Garcia Corporation. We deal with wines and sherries, not flowers flapping about in water."

TESSA STARED AT the taut muscles of Joseph's face and wondered if she'd ever talk to him if he wasn't her brother.

'I do know the difference," she said.

"Then act as if you do!" he snapped. "Women do not go around lifting heavy crates of bottles. There is a difference between smelling perfume and sampling sherry. Do you understand the difference?"

"Don't shout at me!"

"Then let Papa get on with running the business as he thinks fit. Don't act as if you know better than he does. He has run this company for over thirty years—without your advice. You make me ashamed!"

"Why? Wanting to work isn't wrong, and I've never criticised Papa. You're not the only one who loves him, you know."

"There? You see? Only a woman would bring love into it. I'm talking about respect."

"I respect him."

"You respect that François Coty more."

"Don't be so horrid, Joseph, that's different. I suppose it would never occur to you to respect me. You have no idea of the skills I have. I'm prevented at every step from using them. You haven't a clue how trapped I feel."

"Trapped? You are so selfish. Think of poor Frank sitting in his room all day. That's what I call trapped."

"I know, I—"

"You have a beautiful home, loving parents and brothers. Mariquita worships you. She'd love to *be* you."

"Everyone thinks of me as a silly little girl, don't they?"

"Well, stop behaving like one and they might think different! I can't believe you'll be married in a few months, the way you're acting."

"I'm not getting married. Sandes hasn't asked me, and besides, I'd say no."

"That's your choice, but don't come to me whinging that you've spoilt your life. You have a choice, some people haven't."

"Women don't really have a choice, Joseph, if no-one will give them a job."

"You don't need a job. Open your eyes and see how lucky you are."

"Needing isn't only about money."

"What else is there?"

Silence.

"Is that it?" she eventually said. "Even after I've begged?"

"I'm not going to help you play at life."

"I wish I didn't belong to this family. Then I'd be free to go out and prove myself!"

"That comment really shows how naïve you are. Sandes will be much better off without you."

Her palm swept across Joseph's cheek. After a moment, he put his hand up to cradle the hot patch on his face.

"Don't ever do that to anyone—ever again," he said before turning and marching down the aisle of crates, leaving Tessa standing in the vast, cold warehouse listening to the echo of his footsteps.

Chapter Nineteen

T HE RAIN GUSTED in squalls. It bounced out of the torrents flowing along the gutters at that side of the road, in puddles that had formed on the pavements and spouted out of broken drainpipes. Head down, Tessa dodged her way, splashing her stockings and soaking her shoes before, eventually, squelching up the front steps. Water dripped from the brim of her hat, her cuffs and the hem of her coat. The ache of being so wet already pressed into her bones, and she couldn't wait to run a bath and cuddle up with a cup of hot chocolate.

There was no escape; rain even spotted into her purse as she fumbled for her door key. With a shaking hand, she slotted it into the lock. Her numb fingers, stuck inside her gloves, wouldn't make it turn. Tears of frustration rose up. Her dreams, passions—selfishness, as Joseph called it— were all being flushed away. She kicked the hard wood of the door.

As she stumbled over the threshold, she gazed in disbelief at three elegantly dressed figures standing directly in her path. Worse still, one of them was Sandes, and some unknown woman was standing with her brother. Matty was the first to speak.

"Where on earth have you been?"

"You're wet," said Sandes.

She opened her arms. "It's raining!"

"I've never seen anyone drip so much," said Matty.

"Well, I'll get out of your way."

She attempted to shuffle past them, avoiding looking at the extremely elegant woman who hovered behind the two men like a shimmering butterfly.

"Hold on one second. Let me introduce you." Matty stepped aside. "This is Elizabeth Browne. Elizabeth, my sister, Teresa Garcia."

Elizabeth held out her dry gloved hand.

Tessa raised her wet one. "Are you sure?"

When Elizabeth smiled and maintained the offer of her hand, Tessa took it and gave it a firm shake, impressed that Elizabeth didn't show she felt the damp seeping through Tessa's glove or attend to the drops of rainwater that pattered onto her silk evening attire from the brim of the large hat.

"Mary has a cold," said Matty.

"She was wise to stay at home. It's horrible out," Tessa said, moving towards the stairs.

"No, you don't understand. She can't come to the theatre…"

"We've got four tickets," said Sandes.

Tessa paused, understanding the inference.

"Why don't you ask Mariquita?"

She couldn't help but smile at Matty's expression, but she wasn't about to make any sympathetic gestures. One step and she was within reach of the stairs. A few more steps and she'd be in the bedroom, taking off the wet coat and all her other clothes, and then she'd be in a bath and once that worked its magic, she wouldn't die of pneumonia.

"It's no fun with only three," Matty said. "I'll be a gooseberry!"

She stopped, foot almost touching the bottom step, a sharp repost on the tip of her tongue.

"As you've noticed, I'm wet," she said as calmly as she could manage. "Not fit for polite society, and if I don't get out of these clothes, you'll find it's no fun going to your sister's funeral."

"Oh, don't be dramatic. You don't want to let down *Dear Brutus*, do you? He'll be dreadfully disappointed," Matty persisted.

"Of course you must change and get dry." Elizabeth stepped forward. "But Matty says you haven't seen the play, and everyone should see it. I can't believe there is anyone left in London who hasn't seen it. It's been at the Wyndham's for years! You'll feel much better when you change. We have time."

Elizabeth looked at the two men.

"Yes, go! Go get changed!" Matty gestured.

Sandes was the only one not pushing Tessa to come. She shook her head, spraying a chandelier of droplets. Immediately, he pulled a handkerchief from his chest pocket and handed it to Elizabeth, who took it and dabbed the stretch of bare arm above her long glove. Elizabeth lifted her chin and pressed the white cotton to her smooth neck while Sandes' followed the movement of the handkerchief.

Tessa hated the way that made her feel. His attention was not on her but fixed on Elizabeth Browne in her feather-light, dove-grey silk and lace. Elizabeth Browne with her blue eyes shining like clear pools on a summer day and her meadow-fresh perfume wafting light as goose down.

The hem of Tessa's coat dripped with a resounding squelch, to her ears at least, making her acutely aware of the difference between their appearances.

"You'll hurry, won't you?" Matty pursued.

Elizabeth radiated sweetness and light. "We want you to join us."

"You'll be quick, won't you?" Matty said. "Curtain up and all that."

She put her hand out towards the balustrade. She needed to feel the firm security of the polished wood. It was safe. It knew her. It would lead her upstairs.

"Would you like Matty to ring for your maid?" Elizabeth said, her concern as thin as the stair runner. Tessa's coat drowned her. Her knees bent involuntarily. Her head weighed too heavy for her neck, and she felt the pull of the floor.

"Perhaps you should start by taking this off?" suggested Sandes, holding the shoulders of her coat.

"Abigail!" called Matty.

Abigail took the coat away, the door to the servants' quarters swinging shut behind her.

"She'll be coming back straight away, won't she?" Elizabeth asked.

Spurred into action, Matty followed Abigail, leaving the hush of the hall. Elizabeth raised her eyebrows. The stairs towered like a mountain. It took Tessa a second to realise that her blazing cheeks weren't flushed with embarrassment. It was no coy blush at feeling excluded. It was the flash of anger that Sandes was attentive to this tall, fair, beautiful female. Her suitor. Her lover. Her ex of all these things that had made him special to her and she to him.

In that moment, she knew why red roses were the symbol of love. She knew that love did not equal the youthful pink rose or the innocent white. It was not pastel or pretty or clean. It was red, a dark, thickly red, because it was knowing and jealous and passionate. Her temple beat as strongly as her chest thumped. She flushed like a long-stemmed, thorny, red rose and she knew exactly why.

Matty stood poised in the doorway after making a silent re-entrance. With her hand now firmly on the balustrade, and her feet on the first tread, she faced the trio. She sensed the power of her glowing cheeks and dark, sparkling eyes over them, and she didn't need to utter a word.

Mariquita met Tessa in the doorway to their room. The words hung unspoken on her lips as she moved aside. This was not her younger sister who sat at the bottom of the stairs waiting for the morning post. It wasn't the girl who paced the hall as the rest of the family ate breakfast. It wasn't the assassin either, who desiccated the flower displays and brought their mother's wrath down on her head. This was definitely not the person for whom she hid in the deepest recesses of the wardrobe.

"Will you help me?"

Mariquita followed this unknown woman whose glittering eyes and blood-filled cheeks drew her forwards. She helped her sister undress. She patted her skin dry and helped her into an evening gown. She combed her wet hair.

"Maybe you should cut it off for me," Tessa said, looking at her sister's reflection in the dressing table mirror.

Mariquita reached for the hairpins and rolled the thick hair into a low knot.

Tessa touched her crucifix. "Do you know Elizabeth Browne?"

"I saw her arrive, but I didn't speak to her."

"Do you think she looks like a woman in love?"

Mariquita picked up the hairbrush that she'd dropped in her surprise.

"It takes a second to fall in love," Tessa added.

"You make it sound like a deep pocket in an oversized winter coat."

"You merely have to slip in your fingers. Your hand slides inside and then you are up to your elbows, and it's thick and warm and endless. You fall in completely and you know you're safe. You feel its warmth through the wool, and you want to stay there forever."

Chapter Twenty

ALL THOUGHT OF having blazed with jealousy disappeared when Tessa watched the curtain rise to reveal the stage. It remained dark and unlit, but through French windows at the back, a striking view of a garden bathed in moonlight appeared. Through a door on the right, a lit dining room could partially be seen. Through this door, the first actress entered. A jolly, older lady, followed by a younger woman, then three more women, emerged onto the stage.

Later, when all the male characters had joined the women, Tessa, totally enthralled, leaned closer as if she too wanted to enter the garden through the French windows. The drenching rain, Elizabeth and Sandes, her flushed cheeks and powerful emotions were all forgotten.

"They say—that in the wood—you get what nearly everybody here is longing for—a second chance," announced a character called Lob.

"So that's what we have in common!" said Joanna.

"Ahhh!" they all sighed.

"You know, I've often thought, Coady," said Mr. Coade to his wife, "that if I had a second chance, I could be a useful man instead of just a lazy one."

"A second chance!" sighed Mrs. Dearth.

RUTH ESTEVEZ

IN THE FOYER during the interval, Tessa could not contain herself.

"Is the wood magic?" she asked.

"Should we tell her and put her out of her misery?" said Matty.

Sandes stood back, a little wary. "Don't you want to find out for yourself?"

"We cannot tell you," interrupted Elizabeth. "That would spoil the second act, and then you may as well go home."

"But a second chance? Please. Feel free to tell me, please," Tessa begged. "It will still feel a surprise as they'll use different words to yours, and gestures. They'll make it sound completely different."

"You're right, Elizabeth, don't tell," said Sandes. "Tessa wouldn't thank anyone. She may even be angry..."

Tessa fanned herself with her programme. She wanted to be back in her seat, see the curtain rise, be transported back into the garden and that other world of promise.

"My poor sister didn't get to see any plays at the convent. You've got a lot of making up to do, haven't you?" Matty nudged her elbow.

"It really is hard to believe that everyone hasn't seen this play. It's been out so long." Elizabeth gazed at the assembled theatregoers, sipping their drinks, chattering, alert, in case anyone was looking at them.

"Tell us, Sandes," said Matty, "how come you've escaped seeing it before? I feel I've been dragged here at least twenty times!"

114

"There's only one reason," he said, looking over Tessa's head.

"Guess where we were this afternoon?" Elizabeth interrupted before he could elaborate.

"Somewhere new?"

"Harrods," Elizabeth announced. "Sandes wanted to make a few special purchases."

"Secret, rather than special," Sandes amended.

"Oh, yes?" said Matty.

Elizabeth beamed at them. "Sandes bought me a little something, didn't you, Sandes?"

She kept saying his name. It sounded different on her tongue, not belonging to the Sandes Tessa knew. A different person. It made her feel like a different person too, a person she didn't like, who wanted to ram her programme down Elizabeth's throat to stop her saying his name. Instead, she handed her glass to Matty.

"Should we be going back in?"

"Wait until the lights dim, then we can go back. We don't want to be in there when we can be out here," said Elizabeth. "And I want to tell you what Sandes bought for me. You'll be so jealous. It was a bottle of Guerlain! The newest! It is divine!"

Guerlain. Now Tessa knew why Elizabeth Browne seemed so different from herself. "Sandes wouldn't have chosen that." The words were out before she could stop them.

"He absolutely did."

Tessa shot him a glance, but he didn't meet her eye.

"I'm wearing it now. Would you like to smell my wrist?"

"No, thank you."

"Oh, you do…"

"No, honestly. Thank you, I prefer Coty."

Elizabeth laughed. "Really? I guess some people like him, but I much prefer Guerlain."

The bell rang again, and they looked around at the empty bar. Elizabeth raised her glass to her mouth and tipped back her head. Almost immediately, she began to cough. Sandes lifted the glass from her fingers and put it on a table before sweeping one arm around her shoulders. She bent forwards, clutching her throat.

"Please, a glass of water," Tessa asked the barman.

Matty swept it up and handed it to Elizabeth, who gulped greedily.

"You need to sit," ordered Sandes.

He led her to a seat. An usher approached and tentatively suggested they return to their box, but Sandes gestured him away. Elizabeth had begun to cough again. He held out the glass to Matty and ordered a refill.

"You go back in," he said to Tessa. "I don't want you to miss the play when you're enjoying it so much. Thanks." He took the glass from Matty. "Go! We'll join you when we can."

Matty shook his head. "I've seen this thing a thousand times, and once was enough. You go with Tessa. I'll stay with Elizabeth. You said yourself you've never seen it, and why should you be let off with that?"

"I'm fine," Elizabeth insisted but started to cough again.

"I'm sorry, madam," said the usher who had remained close by. "I must suggest that you stay here until you feel better. I'm afraid your cough will distract the audience members near you."

"Nonsense!" Elizabeth spluttered.

"He's right," said Matty. "It wouldn't be fair on the actors either. They've enough to contend with, all those old dodderers snoring. Your coughing would really destroy the actors' concentration."

"That's rather rude."

"But true. Don't worry, though, I will be here."

"Thank you, Matty," Sandes said, "but Elizabeth is my guest this evening. I will remain with her."

Elizabeth sank back into her chair, closing her eyes.

"Sandes!" admonished Matty, sitting next to Elizabeth. "Go back in before it's too late. I cannot possibly watch actors moaning about lost lives and wishing they'd done things differently even one more time."

Sandes looked at Elizabeth as another fit of coughing shook her. Matty waved them impatiently away, and the usher hurried them to their box.

Aware that all around her other people were sitting quietly, Tessa gazed at the action on the stage, although she couldn't help but contemplate his presence to her left. If anything, it spoiled her enjoyment of the play, and she wished Matty hadn't been so adamant. She concentrated as hard as she could on the stage that had been transformed into the wood previously glimpsed through the French windows of Lob's home. The painter, Dearth, stood at

117

an easel and a young girl, his daughter, Margaret, stood nearby.

"Do you think I am sometimes *too* full of gladness?" Margaret asked.

"You are sometimes running over with it," her father replied.

"To be very gay, dearest dear, is so near to being very sad."

"How did you find that out, child?"

"I don't know. From something in me that's afraid. Daddy, what is a 'might-have-been'?"

"A 'might-have-been'? They're ghosts, Margaret! I daresay I might-have-been a great swell of a painter instead of just this uncommonly happy nobody—or again, I might-have-been a worthless idle waster of a fellow."

"You?"

"Who knows? Some little kink in me might have set me off on the wrong road. And that poor soul I might so easily have been might have had no Margaret. I'm sorry for *him*."

At that thought, it washed over Tessa that she was letting Sandes pour through her fingers. She thought of him swearing to love her until death parted them. She clutched her hands together in the hope that by concentrating on them, she'd hold herself still and not reach out to touch him.

On the stage, the lights dimmed and the trees became more obscured. The sound of a nightingale rang out, further away than before. The young girl, Margaret, was counting to one hundred. She ran panic-stricken to the centre of the stage and then from tree to tree. With fear in her voice, she called out.

"Daddy! Daddy! Daddy! Daddy, come back! Come back, Daddy!" She turned, a beam of moonlight shining on her face. "I don't want to be a might-have-been!"

The moonlight faded, and the curtain came down. Tessa sat, wondering what might-have-been could be worse: losing her daddy or never having existed at all. If given the choice, what would she choose?

Sandes offered his large, white handkerchief. She looked down as it tickled her fingers. Elizabeth had used this handkerchief a few hours earlier, and now he held it for her to take.

"I'm not crying," she said.

"No, but you might."

She took it and dabbed her cheeks. The lights in the auditorium were going up, and she squinted at the glare. It had been no time at all. The act had been so short. Too short. And yet it felt as though something momentous had happened.

Sandes pulled her chair around, and wobbling, she managed to right herself.

"What are you doing?"

He dragged his chair around to face her and leaned forward. With her back to the auditorium, she could see only him and the entrance to the box. She held out the handkerchief, but he shook his head.

"What did you think of the play?"

At that moment, it made her think of her father, but before that, she had thought of Sandes, and she couldn't tell him that, not with him staring at her. But still, a second chance at life. Who wouldn't want that?

"I would never have thought of thinking what *might have been*," she said. "I don't usually think about things like second chances. I thought you did one thing, and that was done, then another, then another, without ever thinking about them again, and that was it. That was life. You could never go back and change anything, only forward. I never wondered how I'd do things if I had a second chance, only that I must make a fresh chance. I suppose it's set me thinking, and that's a good thing for a play to do, isn't it?"

"Is there anything you would do differently?"

She wanted to fling herself at him and say, *"Yes! Yes!"* but she didn't. She didn't look at him. She twisted the handkerchief instead.

"I believe in giving people second chances," he said.

"Whether they deserve one or not?"

"Everyone deserves one."

He breathed heavily. So close. She couldn't keep her breath silent.

"Only if they've messed up the first time around," she said.

He put out his hand and took hold of the handkerchief, sliding it from her knee. She grabbed hold to pull it back. She needed it. She needed to hide behind the square of cotton. She tried to stand, but his hands remained close to hers on her lap, the handkerchief tangled between them.

"What about the others? They'll wonder where we are. Elizabeth will have stopped coughing. Matty will be ordering us a drink."

"I know you feel you're not ready," Sandes said, ignoring her words. "But I can wait. I don't want to wonder what might have been with you."

"I can't."

"Please say, one day, I can be more than a friend."

"Elizabeth?"

"She is a friend."

"But why? I've been unkind."

"You weren't unkind. You were unsure, but I think something in you has changed. You seem different. On the stairs, the way you looked... It's all right to change your mind. One word and we'll be back and not asking what might have been."

His face blurred in front of hers. She blinked hard and her vision cleared. She *was* different. Being so cold made her yearn to be warm, but she couldn't find the right words. He knelt down, releasing the handkerchief and sliding his hands around her ribs. Putting a hand on his cheek, she leaned forward and kissed him. Words didn't matter. It was touch that told someone else what was in one's mind.

Chapter Twenty-One

TESSA DID FEEL different, and it didn't bother her that Joseph made no mention of her request or what he would call her outburst. She didn't care anymore if Miss Havers had taken her place as her father's assistant, nor did she care about Mariquita's unspoken thoughts. None of that seemed important anymore. Sandes came to the house as if he'd been coming there all his life. They partnered up with Matty and Mary, walking in the park, went boating and on outings, and no-one mentioned Elizabeth Browne.

Tessa liked Mary. Mary had an infectious laugh that bubbled at the slightest provocation. She might have been Matty's twin, they were so alike in their outlook of wide-eyed innocence and fun. They would be like children when they were eighty, surrounded by pets and grandchildren and still holding each other's hands.

Sandes, in contrast, seemed extremely grown-up, and he intrigued her. Despite that, even now, she could have given him up to have her brother back and to run over the hills with Alfonso, laughing and squealing as speed overtook them. But this warm evening, she could hold his arm, promenading through the park's rose garden, one of many similar couples, and know he would be happy for them all. She liked the park in the evenings, without nannies pushing prams and calling to young children running across the grass. Fewer dogs. Fewer ducks, definitely less noise. Fewer distractions of any kind, it seemed, save those of Sandes trying to snatch a kiss.

They watched Matty and Mary wobble as they stepped into a rowing boat. She and Sandes had already taken one and floated halfway across the water. He took the oars and rowed swiftly, while others dawdled. She lounged back, dragging her fingertips through the cold, green water to cool her passion, she told herself.

Back on land, he appeared more relaxed and less competitive, nodding to people walking in the opposite direction, exchanging pleasantries and enjoying a slower pace. When they heard the band and then saw the dancers, Tessa would not be put off.

"I didn't step on your toes, did I?"

"No," she laughed, "but I think you're better at rowing than dancing!"

The nuns had not prepared any of the girls for dancing with a man. She had danced with tall girls, short girls, well-rounded and bony girls. She had been the youngest and the eldest. She had even danced with nuns, but she'd never danced with a man before. As in a man, not a male relative. He had not stepped on her toes, but the shock of the sensation of their feet brushing against each other's meant he might as well have. Unprepared, too, for the force of leadership when he directed her in the waltz, for the reach to his shoulder and the strength of his grip, she had momentarily flinched. Then the music had surged around them, and conscious of his hand supporting her back, of his other holding hers, and that she was suspended between both, she had allowed him to steer her. Her feet stepped across the ground, mirroring his, her legs stretched to reach his, her shoulders opened, and her entire body moved closer to this man than it had ever been to any other than a family member.

She hummed to herself, his name flowing into her thoughts.

One, two three, Sandes, two, three.

She felt as though they moved as one, flowing together, deciding together, each instinctively knowing how the other turned. The violins twirled them in a way she had never danced. The only requirement was the music. It sounded old-fashioned, she knew that, but that made it all the more romantic. She didn't want to be chic and modern. She wanted to glide amongst women in swishing skirts and men with roses in their lapels.

She glanced up to find he was looking down at her.

"All right?" he asked.

She nodded. Yes. More than all right. Wonderful.

The waltz ended all too soon, and they applauded until the band struck up again.

"Another?"

As they came together again, they became aware of another couple walking towards them and then a familiar voice bidding them a good evening.

"You remember my brother, don't you, Sandes?"

A familiar, tall, blonde, immaculately dressed Elizabeth Browne stood before them.

124

"Edward, let me introduce Miss Teresa Garcia. y brother, Edward Browne."

They all politely faced each other as the music and dancers moved around them.

"May I have this dance?" Edward Browne held out a hand. Tessa glanced at Sandes, annoyed they had been interrupted.

Elizabeth smiled. "I don't mind you taking my partner if Sandes isn't averse to waltzing with me? I'm sure Sandes and I will try our best to bear it."

Sandes and I. The words buzzed in the air. *Sandes and I*, as though they were an engaged couple. She sensed she was being manipulated, but before she could decline, Edward placed his hand on her back and spun her away.

He was slighter than Sandes, more like her brothers. He seemed harmless, and she could have easily escaped his hold if she'd wanted. Straight away, he began talking as if he'd saved words up overnight, and she found she couldn't remain angry for long. He was trying, trying hard to please, telling her all the latest news and taking her deep into the crowd.

"I hear you travel a great deal?" he said, properly catching her attention.

She looked at his pleasant face. He really hadn't a clue why his sister wanted them to dance together.

"Where did you hear that?" she asked.

"It's not true?" He smiled suddenly. "Wait until I speak to that sister of mine."

Tantalisingly, the others appeared and disappeared and reappeared through the crowd again. They were laughing and looked as if they knew each other extremely well.

"You obviously enjoy dancing." Edward spun her away, but it was too late. Tessa had seen Sandes' fingers splayed across Elizabeth's delicate back. She had noticed how his head bent to hers and her face to his. She saw how their eyes held each other's and that their lips mirrored their smiles and how their laughing, open mouths breathed in the same breath. She couldn't speak. She felt anger surge through her limbs.

"Are you well?"

No. She was far from well.

"A little warm. Would you mind if we sit down?"

He led her to vacant chairs that circled the dance area.

"I'll fetch you a cool drink."

Edward left her watching the swirling figures. Within moments, the three of them looked down on her. In her effort to rise, the chair wobbled, and Edward caught her arm, helping her stand.

"Perhaps you should remain seated," said Elizabeth. "This heat does not suit everyone."

"It's not the heat." She accepted the glass Edward held out to her. "Thank you. You are very kind."

"Nonsense," said Sandes. "It's nothing to do with kindness. Edward's feeling guilty that he's such a bad dancer he's made you dizzy. He should be thanking you for not pointing it out."

They all laughed. The tables had turned. She sipped the water, and Sandes continued to gossip with the Browne siblings, who made him laugh at the stories they told of the people they all knew. She didn't know the people they spoke about or care for gossip.

"I think I should return home," she said.

"So soon?"

"If I want to dance tomorrow, I must save my feet today."

Edward bowed. "I hope you will forgive my clumsiness and not hold it against me."

"Of course. And it wasn't you. It always takes two."

"Always take a gentleman's apology," said Elizabeth. "It is most likely their fault anyway, and I'm certain with Edward, that was true. Your role is to help him improve, through your patience and perhaps more practice if you could bear it."

Her blue eyes twinkled. Edward bowed again.

"Thank you. I'll remember that."

Sandes took Elizabeth's hand and kissed her knuckles. Elizabeth smiled. She was beautiful, the evening sun shimmering gold on her hair, eyes sparkling, skin glowing. And then the brother and sister were turning, and Elizabeth waved goodbye.

"Are you feeling any better now they have gone?"

She couldn't tell if he was teasing or not.

"It was remiss of me to keep you out in this heat so long."

"I told you, it's not the heat."

"Then an allergic reaction to Edward, perhaps?"

He really was teasing now, but she couldn't see the humour. She'd lost it somehow, and another sensation had taken its place.

"You can go with them if you like," she said. "I will be fine with Matty and Mary. I see them over there."

He looked truly hurt, and she regretted her sharp words.

"Why would I want to do that?" he asked.

She wanted to stop. She wanted to soften and be light and sunny, but they'd hurt her. He'd hurt her.

"I'm sorry I can't make you laugh the way Elizabeth Browne can. I'm sorry I don't know the same people to talk about."

He studied her face. "You can't possibly be jealous, can you?"

"Of course not."

"What about me? Should I be jealous? What did you and Edward talk about?"

"It's natural you talk about people you both know. You've known the Brownes longer than we've known each other."

"I've never kissed Elizabeth at the theatre."

Kissed. Secretly. Quietly. Making her want more. But that thorny rose wouldn't go away.

"I'm sure you've kissed her elsewhere. I'm sure you've kissed her Guerlain-scented neck!"

It was too late to hide her anger. He didn't say anything but took her arm and led her towards the rose garden. It was the very last place she wanted to be right then.

Not amongst roses. Not amongst thorns where she'd lose herself.

They stopped by a bright-pink bloom.

"I kissed Elizabeth here," he said.

Tessa hadn't expected him to have actually kissed Elizabeth Browne, much less to admit it, and she pulled her arm free. He caught her hand and lifted it to his lips.

"This is how I kissed her. On the hand. Saying goodbye when I told her I loved you."

Chapter Twenty-Two

CARMEN WATCHED THE tired-looking priest leave the confessional box even though a penitent still remained behind the adjacent door. Once the footsteps died away, Carmen opened the door, crept inside and sat down. In the dark, she sensed the person move.

"I love you," she whispered.

"Who's that?"

"Carmen Garcia."

"Do you know who I am?"

"Pierre Roman."

HE HELD HIS breath. What should he do? What did she want? He knew what he wanted. He wanted to run and never look back. The noise of the door opening, his boots on the stone flags, the creak of the church door would all shout out his sin as he ran. He lusted every day he saw Carmen Garcia, and every night he dreamt of her. He wanted to kiss her plump lips and hold those hips that were so unlike the thin hips of the other girls. He closed his eyes, sensing his downfall, until he felt two small hands reach for his face. A finger pressed his eyelid, then his nose. All eight fingers felt his lips. He let the hands turn his head until breath blew softly into his eyes.

WHEN CARMEN SENSED his warm breath on her face, a deluge of emotion crashed through her. She splayed her fingers over his cheeks and pressed her lips to his. As soon as they touched, she knew what to do. Instinctively, she kissed him like a veteran of kisses.

PIERRE ROMAN SANK into hell. No-one knew, or would have known they were there, but that didn't matter to God. He knew. Soundlessly, they fell, spinning, tumbling, burning in their enclosed black box. In that small, dark space, in the huge cool church, in the calm grounds of a convent in Belgium, they fused into one. Pierre still wanted to run, but this time, Carmen would run with him.

He did not dare to think about their destiny, yet Carmen did not ponder over it whatsoever, and gradually, through Carmen's purity of reason, Pierre let his worries and his visits to the confessional subside.

WHEN PIERRE TOLD Carmen he no longer visited the priest, she was furious.

"How can I tell him about us?" Pierre asked.

"Why should you tell him about us? You only tell the priest about your sins."

Pierre leaned his spade into the earth.

"We are sinning every moment," he said.

"Love is not a sin."

The next day, he sat opposite the priest.

"Forgive me, Father, because I have sinned. I look around me, and I love everyone and everything I see."

131

The priest grasped the edge of his seat. "You have found God."

With God's permission, Pierre visited heaven, no longer hell, every day.

Already diligent, he worked harder than he had ever done before. He replanted seedlings, watered the vegetable plots, scrutinised leaves for parasites, dug the soil over and every evening harvested green beans.

PIERRE'S FATHER WATCHED on as he moved through the convent gardens, proud that his only son would one day take over from him as head gardener. The Mother Superior saw the father's pride and said nothing. Pierre's mother watched too, but in her case, she sighed repeatedly.

IN HER LETTERS home, Carmen spoke of her friends' squabbles, the concoctions of the cook, and how she sang and no-one stopped her. She wrote of how Sister Claude tried to sing louder, but no-one could sing louder than Carmen. She did add that Sister Berthe had suggested she play the piano for the others, but that was before she heard how Carmen played the piano. Carmen did not mention in her letters that Pierre Roman had painted forget-me-nots on her bare stomach.

She did not omit to write about these moments because she was deceitful; she had not the vocabulary to describe how she felt. She could have described factually what they did, but when she had tried to do that, the actions had become someone else's and not those of Pierre and herself, so she had torn up the page and never attempted a description again.

All she knew was that it was her body and her mind, and she liked what she was doing with both of them.

Between the hours of two and three, the convent fell quiet. The nuns cowed in personal prayer and the girls in private reflection. They all dreamt of love in whatever form it took.

Carmen did not have to attempt to pass the sentry on the chair by the door of the dormitory because she had never entered her cell in the first place therefore had no need to escape. When the midday meal was over, she slipped out of the line and hid in the cloakroom cupboard. Wrapping the long winter coats around her, she was reminded of the walks in the grounds as the wind sneaked its cold fingers up their skirts and blew back their hoods, exposing their faces. The coats smelt fusty with lack of use in the summer, but Carmen found a use for them. When the washing up was complete, the plates, cups and cutlery stacked away and footsteps stilled, and the convent sank into silence, Carmen let the coats fall to the floor, no longer required, and she emerged into the deserted early afternoon world.

She found Pierre, a solitary figure in the unpopulated landscape of the grounds. Mr. Roman took this hour to rest, Mrs. Roman to darn well-used clothes. Pierre did not see her at first. He stood, legs apart, surveying the poultry in the animal pens. A rabbit hopped by his foot and sniffed his muddied shoelace.

Silently, Carmen opened the wire door and stepped inside the pen. Slowly, she closed it and tiptoed towards

Pierre, whose eyes were fixed on a large, white goose. Undeterred, her fingers crept around his waist, and he jumped, catching her hands. He looked angry and shocked and confused, all wrapped in one glance, but Carmen smiled him into being the Pierre she needed.

"Why are you here?" he whispered.

She touched the top button of his shirt, but he held her hands still.

"I have to catch a goose," he said. "It's for your supper."

Carmen looked across at the half dozen geese with rabbits nuzzling around their feet.

"I will help you."

He pointed to show her which way to approach as he skirted the chosen one from behind. Another hissed. Carmen stepped carefully over a rabbit. Pierre expertly grabbed a long neck and, swooping up the body, sent a flurry of white feathers scattering. Hoisting up the goose, he tucked it firmly under one arm. With his other hand, he held the beak closed and nodded to Carmen to open the enclosure door. Pulling the bolt so that the rabbits, ducks and other geese could not escape, she followed Pierre amongst the trees towards a bleached table bearing cloths, sheets of newspaper and a well-used knife. The wooden handle of the knife was faded and cracked but the blade gleamed sharp.

"I'm going to pass the goose to you."

Carmen looked at Pierre in disbelief. "I can't…"

"I'll hold the beak. It won't snap at you."

She swallowed. He pressed up beside her and nodded for her to open her arms. She felt its body sensing the grip on it was loosening and that here was its chance of escape.

"Keep your arms over the wings," he said as he extracted his hold.

One white wing unfurled. The strength of its heavy body pressed against her. The bone of the wing curved powerfully, its hard edge hitting her face as the goose flapped furiously, its feet pushed against her ribs. Pierre held the beak as the neck arched, and Carmen caught the blackness of its eye. Pierre folded the wing, and Carmen pressed it down with her arm and held the softness of the goose's belly until it remained still. Immediately, Pierre picked up the knife and stuck the point straight into the goose's temple. He spun the handle around, wriggling it into the goose's brain. The goose spasmed, then shuddered. Every sinew in its body struggled. Tears poured down Carmen's cheeks, but she held it firmly right until the moment it stopped moving.

Eventually, Pierre let go of the beak, and the long neck fell limp. He lifted the body from Carmen's arms and hung it from a nail already hammered into the trunk of an apple tree. With bloodied hands, he held her as she sobbed. It was at that point they decided to elope.

During the following weeks, Carmen smuggled clothing, spoons, knives, a couple of plates, mugs and other useful objects, one at a time, into an unused woodshed. Over that final fortnight of the school year, the nuns' hold slackened as packing began for the long summer break when they would all go home.

The final morning before the exodus, as Pierre pushed a wheelbarrow of potatoes past the classroom, he heard the choir of sopranos. The windows stood open, and amongst the high voices, he heard Carmen's discordant alto. He smiled. He would kiss her throat later.

The evening brought with it a gentle rain, but the girls in their dormitory did not care. They would not see each other for two months, and there was a great deal to exchange before their departure. Carmen was the only one to stare out of the window at the foliage as it hung heavy with the persistent shower and the air grew dark with violet clouds.

As night descended and the excited girls, one by one, fell into a restless sleep, Carmen slid out of bed and dressed. She climbed onto the broad window ledge and threw down her small case. Pierre retrieved it from the bushes while she lowered herself amongst the sodden plants, her cape brushing over the greenery. Pulling up her hood, she glanced back at the open window, deciding not to push it closed but to let the sleepers taste the night air. A moment later, hand in hand, they walked down the shining garden path.

A horse and cart stood by the gates. Pierre climbed up, then held out his hand and drew Carmen beside him. Pulling a cover over their heads, Pierre jerked the reins and the horse moved forward. Neither said a word. Neither of them looked back.

Chapter Twenty-Three

EARLY THE FOLLOWING morning, the ringing telephone wrenched Mrs. Garcia out of her stupor. The boys tumbled over themselves to answer it first, and both sisters expected news that Carmen's journey home had begun. They all waited while Mr. Garcia listened to the voice at the other end of the line.

With growing alarm, they watched him turn pale, and when he told them the news, Mrs. Garcia sat with an enigmatic smile on her face. Mariquita's moustache remained rigid over her tight lips while Tessa paced up and down until Joseph ordered her to cease and Matty grasped her hand to prevent another step.

Later that same morning, Joseph and his father stood on the deck of a boat crossing the North Sea. The deep, grey waves rose and fell, making them hold tightly onto the railing.

"No-one will know, Father. We'll nip this in the bud," Joseph said before heaving over the side.

Mr. Garcia glanced at his eldest son spewing up the breakfast he had eaten earlier and he stepped away.

AT HOME, MARIQUITA pressed and folded all the sheets and pillowcases in the linen closet. She sewed muslin lavender bags and filled them with the latest dried flowers. The boys, all as one, gathered around the dining room table, pounding it and shouting over each other for retribution from this presumptive foreign blaggard.

A FORTNIGHT LATER, on his return, their father would speak to them of choice, and although some of Carmen's brothers would never mention her name again, Mr. Garcia would sit in his study and imagine that Carmen was content with her gardener.

MRS. GARCIA SAT at her dressing table and smiled at her reflection. One daughter gone. Two to go. At last, she could glimpse freedom. She decided she had always loved her youngest daughter best.

TESSA AND SANDES stood in the foyer of the office building where he worked. Twelve o'clock chimed on the big bell that dominated the vestibule, and the staff, rushing for their midday break, teemed around them. Sandes steered her towards the emptying lifts; they stepped inside after others had streamed out. He pressed the button for the third floor and the doors closed.

"Joseph and Papa returned last night," she said. "With dreadful news."

"Was your sister with them?"

Tessa touched the side of the lift. She felt stifled. She needed air, and she closed her eyes. She could feel him watching her, but all she could see was her sister standing alone in the pouring rain, her bright hair made dark. She loosened her scarf.

"They could not find her."

"What did they say at the convent? Don't they know where she is?"

"I don't feel well. Can we...?"

The lift was too hot. Sandes stood too close. Someone who was not herself stared back in the metal panels. Then the doors opened, and he steadied her as they walked towards his office where he helped her sit down before handing her a glass of water, which she sipped.

"The man who's responsible for this? What about the Belgian?" he demanded, slamming the door.

She swirled the water around the glass, watching it catch the light. "He's called Pierre Roman," she said. "He worked at the convent. Carmen knew him, and they planned to run away together. Both of them did this. Don't only blame him. Carmen is at fault too."

She put down the glass and walked to the window with its view of the city. It seemed a long time since she was at the convent where nothing had ever happened. She thought of the long, low building and the vegetable gardens. She couldn't recall Pierre Roman. She tried to picture him, yet all she could see again was her sister, laughing this time and running through long grass.

He passed her back the glass of water. "Drink some more."

She raised a hand in refusal.

"Take it. It'll do you good."

She took the glass, but she remained with Carmen in her mind.

Trees, golden amber, glowed in afternoon sunshine. A breeze shook leaves like confetti spiralling into the grass.

A horse whinnied as it pawed the damp earth, its breath snorting through wide nostrils. She breathed in. The damp undergrowth smelt of peat and mulched leaves.

The water flooded tepid down her throat, and through the glass, his face distorted.

"If he worked at the convent, they must be able to trace him," he said. "How big can Belgium be? Someone must have seen them."

"Carmen went willingly, and it seems they have disappeared."

It always amazed her how the truth silenced people. He cleared his throat.

'Your sister is fifteen," he eventually said. "She doesn't know any better. It is a crime in any decent person's book. What does your father say? How may I help?"

He didn't know Carmen. He'd never met her. He hadn't seen her drop her dolls onto the hall tiles to see if they would survive intact. He hadn't heard her confess her thoughts to the priest. Anyone who truly knew Carmen recognised that the girl understood exactly what she was doing from the moment she'd been born.

"They don't want to be found," Tessa said. She couldn't look at him now, but she was unable to block out the tone in his voice or meaning in his words.

"Your father surely isn't letting them do what they want?"

She offered him back the glass, but he strode across the room to stand behind his desk without taking it. He was so unlike her father. This man would bring Carmen back even if she made a logical and reasoned protest.

"There was something one of the nuns told my father," she said.

His face lit up with hope. "They do know where she is? She can be saved?"

Carmen would laugh at that. Carmen didn't believe in being saved. She believed in leaping into the unknown. Putting down the glass, Tessa turned back to the window so that she couldn't see his face.

"She said Carmen was nimble in mind as well as in body."

"What does that mean?"

Down below, people moved about their business, ignorant of this conversation going on above them. It seemed so insignificant what anyone else thought, even what Sandes thought, even what she herself thought. None of it would affect Carmen and her lover.

At the rustle of paper and footsteps, she turned around.

"I'm so sorry, but I have a meeting in half an hour," he said.

"Of course. I wanted you to know, that's all. I didn't want you to hear from anyone else."

"Yes, that was thoughtful, thank you."

"It's not really anyone's business."

"That goes without saying. But you? I haven't asked how you are? Your sister's actions are no reflection on you or your family, although people can act unkindly. You mustn't let it affect you."

Carmen, her younger sister, not affect her? Sandes seemed such a stranger at that moment, someone she barely knew. Carmen, wilful, strong-minded, independent.

Carmen painting, her expression determined. Carmen reaching out her hand as rain streamed down her face. Carmen with Pierre Roman, pulling him towards her and kissing him.

Sandes took her elbow, and they moved towards the office door. He smelt of ink and tobacco, obliterating the aroma of the woods and damp soil.

THAT NIGHT, TESSA soaked in a perfumed bath, locked away from the rest of the house. The lamplight from the bedroom illuminated the small room through the glass-panelled door. Slowly, breathing in the lavender-tinged steam, she raised a leg and ran soap over her calf.

Far away, in Belgium, Pierre Roman caressed her sister's smooth skin. He would be feeling her now familiar body. Tessa wondered what it would be like to be naked in front of a man and what his hands would feel like on her skin. She curved her hand over her knee and tried to imagine it was someone else's touch.

Steam rose from the water. Perspiration trickled down her forehead, and tendrils of hair clung to her face and neck. She wanted so much, and here in London, in this house, she felt her world shrinking rather than expanding. But London, she told herself, was a city of opportunity. She could marry Sandes if she wanted. She could have the intimacy of marriage and the touch of another's hands on her skin.

That is what she wanted, wasn't it? It's what she'd wanted in their kiss at the theatre and in her jealousy of Elizabeth Browne. She rubbed soap over her other leg.

The thorny red rose reappeared, but she couldn't admit she was jealous of her sister. That couldn't be possible, could it?

OUTSIDE THE BATHROOM, Mariquita stepped away from the door. She marched to her bed and picked up one of her pillows and scrunched it tight before throwing it back down. One sister gone and one closing her out. This wasn't the way it was supposed to be. They were three. Gaps weren't supposed to widen between sisters, not sisters like them. Not sisters who stood out the way they did.

Chapter Twenty-Four

HARRODS' PERFUME HALL became a haven. Women meandered in their silks and furs between displays by Guerlain, Elizabeth Arden, Helena Rubinstein, and François Coty. A lady wearing a fox stole around her shoulders strolled from counter to counter, trying lipsticks and creams, powders and scents, never once opening her purse.

Although daytime, chandeliers illuminated the immaculately dressed customers and the perfectly manicured salesgirls. The air tickled with powder-scented particles.

The fox-fur lady reached the Coty display where the assistant stepped from behind the counter, holding a bottle in one hand. Tessa recognised it.

L'Eau de Coty.

The lady repositioned her fur, catching the assistant's arm. As if in slow motion, the bottle spun from the assistant's grasp and arched upwards before it fell, cracking like a bullet on the marble floor. A pool spread around their feet; even at a distance, Tessa breathed in the scent.

The perfume counters disappeared before her eyes. The old lady in the fox fur faded. The distraught assistant melted into the figure of a male assistant, or shop manager, perhaps. He waved his hand dismissively at another gentleman.

"No, thank you, Mr. Coty," he said. "Your perfume will not sell here."

With his erect torso and sleek, blonde head, a young man, not much older than Tessa, raised a slim glass bottle high over his head. He spun around dramatically before hurling the bottle at the tiled floor. A wispy mist rose from the shattered glass lying like miniature islands of ice in the liquid.

Then he winked at her, slowly, unmistakably, as if she were party to some trick. Women surged forward, but he reached out and took her hand. She studied his face, wondering how one eye could be so still and expressionless whilst the other danced with mischief. She'd never seen anyone quite so immaculately dressed, his handkerchief an exact triangle emerging from his breast pocket, his skin as smooth as pressed linen.

The aroma of perfume must be making her hallucinate. This couldn't be real. Female voices clamoured to know the name of the scent that rose from the floor.

"What is it?" the woman in fur demanded.

It wasn't L'Eau de Coty. She'd stepped back in time.

"La Rose Jacqueminot."

"Pardon, Miss?" The assistant, crouched on the floor, looked up.

Tessa let her hand fall by her side. She looked at the inquisitive faces as they emerged from the mist.

"Are you all right, Miss? Are you hurt?"

She searched the faces for that of the perfume maker, but he had vanished with the aroma of his first scent.

LATER THAT AFTERNOON, scented by L'Eau de Coty, Tessa leaned against the balcony of Sandes' apartment, overlooking Lord's Cricket Ground. She hadn't mentioned the incident to anyone. She hadn't mentioned any of her recent imaginings.

She stared down at the figures dressed in white, all of them arranged across the smooth, bright-green grass. The bowler ran, swinging his arm and releasing a leather ball. The batsman tapped it with a crack, and the ball soared through the air like the perfume bottle. She turned away. She didn't want to see it caught.

"I am worried about Papa. He doesn't look well."

Sandes put down his teacup. "It's you I worry about," he said.

"Why? I'm fine."

He treated her differently now. Freer, sure of her. She felt as though she was slipping away and he was stepping inside her body. Teresa Garcia was evaporating, like the perfume in the department store. He was muscling her out of her own flesh so that she no longer existed. She was merely a lingering aroma of other times that would eventually fade. She gripped her hands together so that she felt the hardness of her knuckles and reminded herself that Teresa Garcia stood there in flesh and bone and always would.

He lifted her hand. "It seems as though there are three of us here, not two."

"I see only you and me."

"Mr. Coty is always present."

She couldn't hide her surprise. So he really didn't see her, only another outside force, another person, that he suspected had filled her head, exactly as he wanted to do.

"He's in France," she said. "Not England."

Sandes kissed the spot on her wrist where she'd dropped perfume merely an hour earlier. She had put on too much and had caught the excess by dabbing her neck.

"Is it L'Origan?" he asked.

Matty, Mary and two other figures stepped through the glass doors onto the balcony.

"L'Eau de Coty, that's his latest," said Matty. "If you lived with my sister, you'd know every detail of every bottle that man produces." He nodded towards the pitch. "What have we missed?"

Sandes picked up his cup and saucer and, brushing past them, re-entered the apartment. Tessa could tell there was something wrong and followed into the cooler interior.

"Don't you want to watch the match?" she asked.

"There's not much going on."

She leant against the kitchen counter. "What's the matter?"

He stood at the sink and turned on the tap. "What makes you think anything's the matter?"

"You love cricket. You scrutinise every bowl and strike and wicket, and it's not like you to be unsociable."

He opened a drawer and took out a cloth.

"I'm the host," he said. "We need more glasses."

She smiled. "Glasses aren't kept in there."

He opened another cupboard.

"It doesn't bother me that you didn't know my perfume, you know. Matty only knows because he's always wondering what to buy Mary, and he asks, and I bore him with every detail. How could you know?"

"Things like that matter."

She raised her chin. "Come and smell it again then."

He didn't come over but busied himself with the glasses, so she strolled over to him and raised her chin. He studied her neck for a moment but then turned away and filled the kettle under the tap.

"Don't be like that. I'm only teasing."

She reached across and flicked water at him. Without flinching, he turned off the tap and placed the kettle on the hob before facing her.

"I want to be with you," he said.

She laughed nervously. "You *are* with me. I'm here, aren't I?"

He took her hand and held it flat against his chest. His heart was beating fast.

"That's how you make me feel," he said. "Don't tease my heart. Take it seriously."

His eyes pleaded, and his cheeks flushed. She should have been swept away, swept off her feet, but she froze.

Drawing back her hand, she forced a smile. "I'm monopolising you," she said. "Matty will be in, in a moment, baying for more tea."

They returned to the balcony, where Sandes replenished cups while Tessa watched the afternoon slip away to the sound of bat on ball and men's voices raised in over-enthusiastic commentary.

Chapter Twenty-Five

THE GENTLE LIGHT of morning filtered through the curtains and fell across the room. The activity of the house beat in the background.

Mrs. Garcia lay on the bed and stared at the ceiling. She was dissolving. As she lay, limbs outstretched in the warmth, she felt her body sink. It kept on sinking until the mattress and the covers closed over her and all trace of her existence was eradicated.

The children kept their distance. They were entities to themselves, not needing her guidance. They would not mourn her if she disappeared into the mattress because they had lives to live. Watching them from another world would be no different than listening to them from this.

She stretched out her hand. It was no longer the hand she knew. She was in a body she had no use for. It was best to leave it behind in the bed. She slowly lowered the arm back onto the cover and continued to lie, already opaque, in the house full of someone else's noise.

MR. GARCIA DRESSED slowly and meticulously. He studied his face in the mirror but didn't recognise himself. This was an old man's face. The little boy had run away a long time ago. He buttoned up his jacket, placed a fresh handkerchief in his pocket, straightened his cufflinks and walked downstairs.

His eldest son, Joseph, busied himself at the warehouse already, overseeing the delivery of crates of sherry from the vineyards in Jerez de la Frontera.

Tony and Nacho should have been performing this task today, but Joseph could never rely on anyone else. Tony and Nacho knew that Joseph knew this, so they did not hurry their breakfast, even though Nacho had an uneasy feeling in his stomach.

Frank sat by the window with a cup of coffee in his hands. He drank it slowly, savouring the sugared heat.

No-one asked why Mariquita had woken with such a black cloud over her head. She seethed even more because they did not ask, and she vented her hurt by declaring this a day of spring cleaning. Tessa groaned until her sister's combatant glare aroused rebellion.

AN UNTOUCHED CUP of tea stood on the bedside table as Mrs. Garcia faded into the mattress. Yesterday, she had realised that it wasn't her mind that was playing shadow puppets with her. Yesterday, she had found out for sure that she was a woman who really was no longer of this world. She had sat in her dressmaker's, one she had frequented for many years, waiting for her appointment. She had arrived fifteen minutes early, had declared this and then had waited for Sarah to take her through to the dressing rooms.

Other clients arrived. Sarah talked to them. Sarah talked to the receptionist before disappearing to the fitting rooms. Hours passed and clients came and went, and Mrs. Garcia sat and waited because she thought they were running late. She didn't mind. After all, where else had she to go? Eventually, heart beating fast, she had stood and asked the receptionist if her appointment would be soon. Sarah immediately appeared.

"I am so sorry, Mrs. Garcia. I did not see you there."

Sarah's words stabbed her heart. Sarah had not seen her. Nor had the receptionist. She'd become invisible. That was the truth of it, and she would lie in bed all day and the next, until only her spirit shadowed the house.

TESSA HEARD THE door close and, thinking it was Miss Havers collecting the post, ran into the hallway only to find it empty. She did not realise that Miss Havers, at that very moment, stood in the study reading a letter of recommendation, written in Mr. Garcia's hand, for her future employer while a steaming cup of coffee stood abandoned on the desk.

MINUTES BEFORE, WITH shaking hands, Mr. Garcia had opened a letter from his bank manager, Captain Hatchett, and had read on the single sheet of bank headed notepaper, that he, Mr. Joseph Garcia of the Garcia Corporation for the Importation of Fine Wine and Sherries, was declared bankrupt. He had folded the sheet and returned it to its envelope, requesting a cup of black coffee from Miss Havers.

Whilst his children ate their breakfast and his wife lay in bed, he carefully put the letter in his briefcase, quietly closing the clasp. From the desk drawer, he took out the handwritten letter of recommendation that he had sealed in an envelope with Miss Havers' name on it earlier that week and rested it against her typewriter. Then, dropping a bag of Liquorice Allsorts into his jacket pocket and silently closing the study door behind him, he walked down the hallway, picked up his hat and walking stick and left the house.

TESSA HUDDLED ON the window seat, determined not to stir. Mariquita watched the door swing closed behind Abigail and the last tray of breakfast dishes.

"What is the matter with you?" she demanded.

"Can't you stop being angry?"

"You're the one who sounds angry."

"I'm bored, aren't you ever bored?"

"That's a luxury we don't have. There won't be any time for being bored when you see what we have to get through today."

"How can you sound so cheerful about cleaning?"

"These tasks need to be done, and we have to work through them. There is satisfaction to be had in that."

"But cleaning needs to be done again and again. It's relentless."

"It's our function in life, so you'd better get used to it, and it has its compensations. We'll start in here."

Tessa made her decision right at that moment. She got up and strode towards the door, but halfway past the table, Mariquita grabbed her arm and, with her superior strength, swung her sister around.

"Where do you think you're going?"

"Out!"

"You are not. You're going to do your share right here."

"You can't make me."

"I can stop you behaving like a selfish, spoilt brat!"

Tessa had had enough of being told what to do and what she couldn't do, by her father, her mother, the nuns, Father Ryan, by Joseph and now Mariquita. She lashed out, slapping her sister hard across the left cheek.

MR. GARCIA WALKED down the tree-lined street, his walking stick punctuating his steps. He crossed the shaded road and entered the station where other men, wearing similar hats and carrying similar briefcases, boarded trains and took their seats. He boarded with them as the day of business loomed and listened to the sound of the tracks that carried him towards the city. The light strobed across the features of the commuters. Flash, flash, flash. Click, click, click.

THEY FACED EACH other. Suddenly, Mariquita pounced, grabbing Tessa's upper arms while Tessa grasped her sister's, and they pushed with all their strength against each other. Chairs fell sideways and crashed to the floor as Mariquita forced Tessa to stumble backwards. Without relinquishing her hold, she dragged her sister with her, and they bruised themselves on the table's edge. Tessa pressed her feet hard into the floor, ploughing forwards, pushing Mariquita into retreat.

THE CROWDS TEEMED around Mr. Garcia as he stood outside the station, gauging his surroundings. People rushed with an urgency Mr. Garcia no longer understood. He gripped his briefcase and held his ground.

MISS HAVERS PUT on her coat, positioned her hat and closed her bag. She paused, then crossed the room and sat in the chair usually occupied by Mr. Garcia. She thought of her own home, a small room in a large house where other people rented rooms and shared a dining room and pretended to be interested in each other. She had liked Mr. Garcia and his noisy home. She was tired of the silence in her head. Slowly, she became aware of unusual thumps that were not a part of the daily cacophony.

IN THE DINING room, they glared breathlessly at each other. Mariquita lay on her back, pressed up against the table legs. Tessa sat astride her, skirts rooked up over her knees. Mariquita made one last effort to raise her arms to unpin herself but found she was unable to move. She strained to lift her hips, but Tessa, like a rodeo rider, bore the uprising and pressed her sister's hips back down to the floor.

Leaning forwards, her loosened hair straggled down into her sister's face. They breathed hard against each other, staring the other into submission, when, without warning, Tessa pushed against her sister and levered herself up.

As the door slammed, Mariquita rolled over onto her side and lay in a sobbing heap on the floor.

NOT LONG AFTERWARDS, Mr. Garcia entered Captain Hatchett's office at the bank. The meeting did not take long. Both men knew that Mr. Garcia's accountant had brought about the current state of affairs, but the money had gone with no way to retrieve it. They both decided there was no point in them discussing who was to blame. Mr. Garcia was bankrupt, and it would be the Garcia family's sixty-three-year-old shipping business that folded.

AT TWELVE-THIRTY, MARIQUITA sat alone at the dining table. Her brothers were now all active at the family warehouse. Her mother lay invisible upstairs, and Tessa perched on the edge of Alfonso's grave.

None of them felt the jolt of the train as the brakes slammed down. Not one of them lurched with the passengers or reached out as they ran across the platform to aid the body that had fallen on the tracks.

Mr. Garcia had waited for the train to take him home. He saw it approaching and stepped with the others to greet it. Feeling in his pocket, he realised that he hadn't eaten. Taking out a blue-flecked sweet, he placed it on his tongue and tasted the syrup of the liquorice. Jerez de la Frontera afternoons beckoned, childhood hours where responsibility meant helping his grandmother out of her chair or not complaining when called in to bed at dusk. He turned, caught in the rays of the setting sun, blazing golden on the whitewashed walls, and he slipped. Someone shouted but too late, he had lost his footing. The sweet caught half-dissolved in his mouth, and he opened his hands, letting go of his briefcase. Faces blurred, noise of voices smudged in his ears. Falling. Then the hard stone and cold iron hit hard, and he felt his existence disappear.

On the platform, there remained a crumpled bag and a trail of black-and-white sweets, highlighted only by the odd flash of colour.

Chapter Twenty-Six

MARIQUITA'S ACTION PLAN blasted through the stations of responsibilities without stopping. She ticked off the points on her list as if her life depended on it being done. She conferred with Father Ryan, picked out the casket, hand-wrote cards and sent them out, made sure the entire family had black to wear and that black armbands were stitched. She ordered flowers for the wreaths...did everything it took to hold in tears and kind words.

The Garcia family arrived at the church, falling like dark handkerchiefs from their carriage. Mrs. Garcia stared at Father Ryan for the entire service without needing to blink away a tear. She recognised the man the priest spoke about and felt proud that she had shared his life, but there remained a hollowness in the pit of her stomach not caused by the hunger she should have felt, having eaten no breakfast, but by the not-yet-accepted fact that Mr. Garcia would never again catch her eye or hold her hand. Never again would she hear him ask, *"Where are the children?"* Never again would she have to search for the answer.

Although she felt empty at that moment, beyond the chasm yawning inside her, whispering behind the rock pressing down on her chest, there was a circle of light that promised reprieve. She remembered once, the only other time when she'd felt like this, when the land lay frozen and the vast sky heavy. It had been wintertime and a bitter cold had numbed their limbs. She balanced on the ice-packed soil, looking down at her father's coffin. A sheep bleated. The wind caught the women's black skirts and the men's cloaks. That church from long ago stood empty, but still, she heard the bleak midwinter words.

Mariquita sat beside her in exactly the same upright position. On her left, Joseph stared straight ahead at the altar. They were so alike in their rigidity that the others, slightly slouched, slightly at an angle, appeared as though from a different, more lax age.

SANDES SAT WITH his parents across the aisle. He thought how tiny Tessa looked dressed in black. He didn't like her so sombre and distant. It aged her. It took away the sparkle from her eyes so that they appeared like congealed chocolate. Frank coughed, waking everyone from their thoughts.

TESSA LOOKED AT the wreaths covering the coffin. Mrs. Garcia had said she thought he was smiling when they'd stood in line and viewed the open casket and made their farewells. She had recoiled in shock at the hardening cold of his cheek when she bent to give a last kiss. It was at that moment that she accepted that her father really was dead and that his body lay like a bar of odourless soap in his silken dish.

A white lily stirred. She had insisted on lilies and her mother had agreed. She thought of the drawer with its paper bag of Liquorice Allsorts. She saw the large black typewriter standing silent and unused. She heard the clock and the chime and the muffled noises through the door. Questions bubbled up. Her eyes itched like dry stone quarries, swirling with dust.

Dead. Lost forever, the smiling eyes and words and laughter. It didn't matter that she hadn't seen them for some time; now there was no chance they'd ever be resurrected.

She couldn't think of him falling, only that he was now lying down without breath or movement. Gone, and so many words unsaid. It was for all the lost opportunities she mourned, the chances to ask him things and discover who he used to be. Most of all, she missed the chance to tell him she loved him and for him to tell her he loved her too.

When it came to returning home, she didn't want to leave the graveyard where her father was buried beside Alfonso. The pile of earth had appeared so small, disguised into grandeur by the multitude of stiff wreaths. Sandes remained by her side even though she hadn't asked him. He held her hand, even though she didn't want his touch. Quelling the desire to shout at him to go away, to leave her alone, she held his hand too tight so that he didn't inadvertently make a loving movement.

He, for his part, took her grasp for need and placed his arm across her back. She breathed in at this touch, not from gratitude as he thought, but from anger. Yet she said nothing, and the other mourners thought that the event would bring the young couple's union more speedily to its inevitable conclusion.

Tessa meandered off the main path and into the older part of the cemetery, stepping through the long grass, and Sandes followed. He wanted to take her back to the carriage, to drive to the house and join the other mourners. However, reluctant to question her, he allowed his footsteps to crush hers. A large elderflower was in blossom, and its heavy odour permeated the path, preventing her from disappearing completely into the wilderness. Pollen caught on her hat, and he brushed it solicitously away.

With nowhere to go, she sank onto the ground so that the blades of grass towered around her shoulders and her skirt ballooned like an enormous airship. Glancing back at the cultivated part of the graveyard and finding it obscured from view, he bent in front of her, her skirts deflating beneath his knees. This was a different Tessa to the one he'd grown to know. She seemed to belong amongst the ancient, unvisited graves with the aroma of damp undergrowth mixed with the strong scent of creamy summer. Insects hovered. He waited for her to lead.

"I can't cry anymore," she said.

He nodded. He'd agree to whatever she wanted today.

"I'm hot."

To his discomfort, she began to unbutton her jacket, and he put out his hand to stop her.

"I have to," she insisted.

He glanced away, but within minutes, out of the corner of his eye, he caught the pale blue of her undergarments. She arched and dropped her head back, exposing her bare neckline. Intrigued, he followed her arm as she removed the dark hat and veil and then pulled off the long-sleeved jacket so that she sat only in her silk camisole and old-fashioned black skirt.

She sighed. "That's better."

She ignored him, continuing to act as if she were alone, lying down and flattening the grass. He put his hand against the ground and, finding it cool, felt envious that he did not feel he could join her in finding relief from the sultry air: he thought it best to keep an eye out for anyone who strayed down their path.

"Why don't you take your jacket off?" she suggested without opening her eyes.

He glanced back again at the obscured and now silent cultivated part of the cemetery.

"Your mother will be expecting us."

She sighed again.

They listened to the insects and breathed in the surrounding sweetness, hoping for a breeze to cool their skin. Eventually, he took off his jacket.

"I've never known it so hot."

He laid it down carefully at his side. Tessa looked as though she'd fallen asleep. She had not moved for some time. A large bee plodded up her arm, swaying under its own weight; Sandes watched its progress. Still, she didn't move, and he didn't want to force it to sting her by trying to remove it.

The bee fumbled its way upwards, pausing before it negotiated her narrow shoulder strap and then tapped its way over the bone at the base of her neck. He held his breath, watching the bee rise and fall as it felt its way over her skin. He wanted to reach for it now, to cradle it in his palm, preventing it from gaining the lace edge of the camisole and disappearing in the cool shadow below. Its legs again tapped her skin, feeling the plumpness after the hardness of her breastbone.

Mesmerised, he held his breath. Then, without warning, the bumblebee took flight, heaving its un-aerodynamic body upwards until it settled on the cream blossoms overhead. Tessa appeared not to have felt its pressure, but continued in her reverie, far beyond his gaze. He leant across and retrieved her dark jacket, folded it carefully and laid it on top of his own. He sighed.

Still no reaction from Tessa, he strolled away in search of distraction in the corroded lettering of the surrounding graves. Pausing before a stone angel with its wings outspread, he noticed for the first time how tired he felt. The childlike face of the cherub stared emotionlessly down at him, and he bent to read the names and the verses, but the letters had dissolved into the corroding stone. He moved through long grass, further away, squinting at the relentless expanse of empty blue overhead and, taking off his hat, fanned his face before retreating under the shade of a large horse chestnut tree. He swore suddenly when his shirtsleeve caught on a bramble and a rogue berry spread a stain on the white cotton.

He looked down at a stone almost entirely covered by ivy, careful now of what could catch him. Pulling at the tendrils that reluctantly released their hold, he bent to decipher the lettering. It was unexpectedly easy to read.

I had a little bird
its name was Enza
I opened the window,
And in-flu-enza.

Jonathan and Sophie Cook
1919

The grasshoppers scratched their legs as flies buzzed over the ladies' lace. Sandes replaced his hat and walked back towards the sweet-smelling corner of faded elderflowers, to find Tessa replacing her jacket and buttoning up the front.

"I was dreaming," she said as he approached.

He swept up his own jacket. "What about?"

She continued to preoccupy herself with the small buttons.

"Was it a good dream?"

She kept her focus on the buttons, and he wondered if she was hiding her tears.

"There was a bee on you," he said in an effort to distract her. "I wanted to brush it away, but in the end, it flew off by itself."

"Where was it?"

"On your arm and here." He touched his tie.

163

"I think I must have felt it in my sleep and that's what made me dream."

"It didn't sting you, did it?"

She shook her head.

The heat was unbearable. He felt a trickle of sweat down his back. She was again unbuttoning the jacket.

"I can't," she said. "It's smothering me."

She tugged at the sleeves, dragging them down her arms. He reached forward and helped her pull, and between them, they threw it to the ground. They stared at each other. The bee buzzed in nearby flowers.

"Is that it?"

"I think so."

They watched the satiated bee feel its way across the creamy blooms.

"I can't do it. I can't put it on again. It's like a straitjacket."

Sandes fanned his hat in front of her face.

"Does that help?"

"Why don't you kiss me?" she asked.

"Here? Now?"

"Yes."

He looked around. "This really isn't the time, not when you're upset."

"Don't you want to comfort me?"

LATER, HE HELPED her into her jacket and then put on his own. They silently retraced their steps, leaving behind the flattened grass and smear of dark juice on a forgotten gravestone that rose out of a skirt of dishevelled ivy.

Chapter Twenty-Seven

S ANDES SAT UNCOMFORTABLY while the two women sewed. The window stood slightly open, but there was no breeze to cool the room. Tessa's needle slipped up and down through the linen. He followed the thread as it formed the knot of a flower. He didn't look at Mariquita, but he was aware that she was watching his every movement.

TESSA CAUGHT HIS eye as the door opened and Abigail pushed the tea trolley into the room. He stood to move the needlework box from her path, but Mariquita's hand reached it before his, and she swiftly swung it to the side, defiantly goading him before slumping back in her chair.

"Will you call Mrs. Garcia, Abigail?" she said.

"Madam gave word she won't come down today," Abigail answered. "She sends her apologies to Mr. Sandes."

"Thank you."

Mariquita poured the tea and they ate the hot muffins and Victoria sandwich cake in silence, and with each mouthful, she suppressed the urge to tell him to depart.

"Why did you stay in the cemetery when we all left?" she eventually asked. "What were you doing?"

Tessa took a sip of tea and didn't answer until she'd put the cup back down.

"Nothing."

"It was hours before you returned to the house. I can't believe you stayed there and did nothing for all that time."

"It was my fault," said Sandes. "My apologies."

"We were looking at gravestones."

"You aren't interested in gravestones! Where did you really go?"

"It's the truth," he interjected. "There were some beautiful verses to read."

"Like what?"

"That children's rhyme about Spanish influenza."

"That wasn't written on a headstone!" burst out Mariquita. "Stop being so frivolous, nobody would have that carved as a memorial."

"Well, it was."

Mariquita flashed him a look that would have shrivelled a fly.

"Stop teasing her," said Tessa.

"I'm sorry." He smiled before looking back at the elder sister. "I did find a stone commemorating two people who had died from influenza. I think they must have been a loving couple who were taken too young."

"What were their names?"

"Jonathan and Sophie Cook."

"They could have been brother and sister, father and daughter, mother and son…"

He glanced at Tessa. She touched her collarbone, remembering the feel of those tiny legs and the sensation of velvet brushing her skin.

"The stone said clearly that they were husband and wife."

Mariquita slurped her tea.

"Don't you think that's romantic?" said Tessa.

"No, I do not, and I don't see why it took you so long to read a couple of gravestones. I had to see to people here. Mama just sat and held court, and I had to make sure—"

"It was hot," Tessa interrupted. "I lay down for a while."

"You did what?"

"The grass was cool. I lay under an elderflower tree."

"It was Papa's funeral and there were people."

"There was no-one else there. We didn't disturb anyone."

"But here. You should have been here. I think that is selfish and completely inappropriate. Mr. Sandes? I am highly disappointed in you."

He bent his head. "I didn't feel it my place to tell Tessa how to grieve. As she says, it was extremely hot, and with emotions running high—"

"Don't tell me she was praying?"

"In a fashion, I suppose."

"Your absence here was noted."

"I'm sure you had everything and everybody under control," said Tessa.

"That's not the point."

Tessa picked up the hot water jug and stood. "I think we need more water."

"I'll ring for Abigail."

"It'll only take a moment." Tessa reached the door. "Abigail is also upset by Papa's death, and I don't want to keep bothering her."

"Oh, give it here," said Mariquita, crossing swiftly to the door and snatching the jug. "He's your guest."

When she left the room, Tessa grabbed his sleeves, then reached for his neck and kissed him. She didn't care, only that he responded by kissing back and holding her tight. The relief made Tessa kiss harder. The touch of the bee, of the long grass, his hands, his fingers, lips, tongue. She'd wanted it; she wanted it all over again. Toast, butter, tea, his hair, her scent, the sheerness of her dress, all caught up in the room.

IT TOOK MARIQUITA a few minutes to refill the jug with boiling water in the kitchen. Returning, she paused, one hand on the door handle. There were no voices within, but she heard an unidentifiable sound. Pressing one ear against the door, she listened to the rustle of fabric. She strained to make out what it could be and, in doing so, let the jug tilt. Boiling water hit her leg and she yelled out.

Grabbing the handle, she pushed open the door. Sandes, caught halfway across the room, stumbled over the needlework box. Tessa fell onto the chair on top of him in a tangled mass of limbs. Spools of thread rolled across the floor, ricocheting off chair legs.

Kicking the reels out of her way, Mariquita marched towards the tea table, ignoring their disarray and the laughter that excluded her.

"Mama's trying to sleep upstairs!" she shouted, the hot water jug still trembling in her hand. "And I bet she hasn't touched her tea!"

LATER, IN THE hallway, Tessa handed Sandes his hat.

"I love you," he said. "I love you, and I want us to be husband and wife."

168

Chapter Twenty-Eight

TESSA DIDN'T HAVE a chance to announce her news the following morning because an item in *The Times* took all their attention. Joseph finished reading and slapped the newspaper down on the table, making knives and forks rattle on half-finished plates of sausages, eggs and tomatoes.

Tony shoved back his chair. "Ten years in prison is pathetic for what that man's done."

Mrs. Garcia rose from the table.

"Thank you for reading us the article. I don't want to hear anymore," she said before leaving the room.

They listened to the creak of the top stair and her bedroom door close before erupting into discussion.

"You are so insensitive, Joseph," said Matty. "You shouldn't have read that out in front of Mama."

Voices contradicted him, but Joseph's voice rose above the rest.

"She had to know what happened to this man, this so-called accountant. Without knowing that he is to be punished, she could not put all the rumours about Father to rest."

IN HER BEDROOM, Mrs. Garcia lay on her bed.

"My life is sliding away," she told herself. "Soon, this will be long ago."

In the dining room, voices grew louder.

"I wish I'd been at the trial," said Tony. "I'd have made sure he'd got fifty years!"

"Sure you would, Tony," said Matty. "That's a death sentence."

"He deserves it for embezzling from Papa. Called himself Papa's accountant. Friend, even. He and his wife have dined at the house, for goodness' sake, and he does this? A death sentence is too good for him!"

"No-one has the right to take another's life," said Mariquita. "You can't demand death sentences."

"He took Papa's life!"

"Papa took Papa's," Tessa corrected.

"Papa fell. He did not take his own life. He fell."

"Shouldn't we be concentrating on this?" asked Tony, stabbing the newspaper until Joseph pulled it away.

"Ten is the usual term for embezzlement," Joseph said. "He has been given the full term for that crime, so we must be pleased he has been found out."

"Thank God for justice."

"Thank the courts."

"I hope he'll never work again if he ever gets out," said Matty.

Joseph folded the newspaper. "He won't."

"Papa seemed distracted for a long time," said Tessa. "Do you think he knew?"

Joseph slammed the newspaper on the table again. "What do you mean, did he know?"

Mariquita took her sister's arm and led her to the window seat. Tessa didn't feel justice had been done.

She didn't know Mr. Jackson, her father's accountant, couldn't equate him with a flesh-and-blood person who had left his wife and children with nowhere to live and probably to be spurned by their relatives and their neighbours because of his prison sentence for bringing about the Garcia family's bankruptcy.

She looked at her brothers, still sitting around the table, elbows next to plates stained with eggs and tomatoes, coffee half drunk, crumbs scattered over the cloth. What did she know of them either, beyond their obvious character traits? Did any of them really know any of the others? They weren't children anymore. They had learned about how people mistreated each other and the effects of that, and it surely altered them all.

She looked from face to face, some filled with shame, others anger and all of them, fatigue. Nacho, as always, looked puzzled. She pictured Frank, sitting in his room, turning the pages of *Peter Pan*, oblivious, wishing he were back in childhood, no doubt, before wars and people turning on each other. Glancing at her sister, she was surprised to see a triumphant attitude in her posture and her black eyes gleaming. It was difficult to understand why each of them could react so differently once the initial state of grief subsided.

"Mariquita?"

"Yes?"

"Sandes has asked me to marry him," she said. "Does that seem wrong when Papa is dead and Mr. Jackson is going to prison?"

Mariquita frowned.

"You do say silly things at times. It isn't wrong, but you mustn't use it as an escape."

THAT NIGHT, TESSA lay in bed, listening to the regularity of Mariquita's snores and wondering if everything they did in life was an escape. Closing her eyes, she thought of Alfonso pulling a kite behind him as he ran along a beach they had once visited. She could see Carmen painting at the table by the window, big thick sweeps of her brush, the little bottles filled with moulding water and tiny labels with tiny writing. Then she thought of Sandes and the graveyard and the warmth of his lips. Was love an escape?

Unable to sleep, she sat up and, deciding a glass of milk would help, crept into the hall. At the top of the stairs, she paused. A light shone from beneath her mother's door.

INSIDE THE BEDROOM, Mrs. Garcia sat at her dressing table, singing a ballad she'd sung as a child. Singing it, she was little Ann Loughlin again, who wasn't going to change into anyone else when she grew up. When the door opened, she caught her daughter's reflection in the mirror.

"Do you remember me singing that to you when you were small?" she asked, unfastening the pearls from around her neck and placing them in their velvet box.

TESSA CLOSED THE door.

"I remember the scent of lavender after you bid us goodnight."

Before the words were out of Tessa's mouth, Mrs. Garcia grabbed a glass bottle from the table in front of her and hurled it at the wall immediately above her daughter's head. The explosion of glass shocked them both. Pieces of glass tinkled to the floor. Mrs. Garcia didn't say a word.

Slowly, Tessa touched the droplets streaming down the wallpaper and smelt her fingertips.

"Chypre!" she cried out.

Mrs. Garcia hurled another bottle at the door. Instinctively, Tessa reached out to catch it, but it smashed against the wood.

"Emeraude!" Mrs. Garcia announced. She raised a third perfume bottle and threw it at the wall where the first bottle had struck. This time, Tessa leapt forward, her hands outstretched. Catching her toes on the tapestry footstool, and with searing pain shooting up her foot, she fell heavily on her knees, banging her shoulder against a mahogany chest of drawers.

She looked down at the bottle lying intact in her hands. Her shoulder ached and she could not stop the geyser of tears from rising up. Clutching the bottle, she sobbed so hard that Mrs. Garcia knelt down next to her. The clock ticked. The perfume dripped down the walls.

"So there is something you care about," Mrs. Garcia eventually spoke.

"You can replace them."

"No-one can replace wasted years."

"No, I meant—"

"I know what you meant."

Mrs. Garcia leant forward and dabbed Tessa's wet cheeks. "I'm sorry I can't replace your father."

"What happened to him?"

"Life is dangerous. It's easy to fall."

Squeezing her eyes tightly shut, Tessa tried to blot out the image of the train's wheels and the track and the crowds in the station.

"I can't believe he isn't here. I can't believe he won't be in his study asking Mariquita to get him more sweets and I won't taste a Liquorice Allsort ever again."

"It would have been quick. Painless."

"Don't, Mama."

"He wouldn't want you to cry for him."

"I didn't speak to him, not properly, for months. I had things to tell him, to ask him. He thought I hated him..."

"He didn't think that. What did you want to tell him so badly?"

"I wanted him to understand me."

"Ah. Now you know as well as I do, that is always difficult. We don't even understand ourselves, do we?"

Mrs. Garcia lifted the bottle of Emeraude from Tessa's hands and tossed it randomly, until it fell against the mirror on the dressing table. The light glass splintered, and perfume seeped into the cloth.

"Why did you do that?" Tessa asked.

"I'm packing," her mother replied.

Dresses draped across the bed and over a packing case on the floor by the window.

"But why are you breaking your perfumes?"

"I don't want to take reminders with me, and aromas are more evocative of times gone than anything else."

"You'll wake everyone. Mariquita sleeps lightly."

"It's you who needs to wake up, not your sister."

Her mother sat like a child in her nightclothes, with her thick hair hanging loose around her shoulders. She wasn't as old as they'd all assumed. Her skin glowed fresh and her grey eyes shone bright; Tessa wondered if her mother had lost her mind.

Without warning, Mrs. Garcia grabbed Tessa's shoulders and began shaking them. Her fingers gripped tightly, and she shook harder and harder, making Tessa rock back and forth. Tessa tried to grasp her mother's arms and push her away, but she couldn't break free.

"Wake up!" Mrs. Garcia shouted. "Wake up!"

"I am awake! Stop it, you're hurting!"

Her mother didn't take any notice and kept on shaking.

"I'm trying to show you, but you're not seeing."

"What? What am I not seeing? Show me, don't shake me!"

"You don't know what it's like."

Tessa grappled her way free, and they sat, panting at each other.

"I know you didn't love Papa, if that's what you mean," she said. "I know you probably don't love any of us."

"Oh, you silly. D'you think I would be here if I didn't love your papa? That's what I'm telling you. That was my mistake. If I hadn't loved—if we hadn't met even. It's all ifs for me, but you can still wake up. I don't want you to feel as I do."

"I don't. I won't."

"You're in love with Sandes, don't think I don't see it. It's obvious. Why else would you stay behind after the funeral and not come home with the rest of the family? I'm not ignorant of these things. Of course you're in love with that handsome, dashing, charming man. But no-one learns what that means, and I'm trying to tell you."

"Tell me what?"

"That love is our downfall. Don't you see how we lose ourselves? Men carry on being men, going to their offices and their clubs and games. They carry on with their lives like before, but we become someone else. We lose our names. We lose our bodies. We lose our dreams. We become not what we dreamed of being when we were little girls."

"You mean women like us? Not all women?"

"Love is every woman's downfall, no matter who you are."

"I disagree, Mama. It's different now. We do things. We have careers and respect. Sandes loves me, he wouldn't—"

"Oh, Tessa. Don't be naïve."

Mrs. Garcia prised herself to her feet, and Tessa rose to face her.

"He respects me," she insisted. "He's not like Papa. He doesn't mind me working like Papa minded, and I can be myself, whatever I want to do. He wants me to be happy. He wouldn't stop that. Times have changed, Mama. Women can do whatever they want."

MRS. GARCIA LOOKED at her daughter. Hopeful. Eager. Sure of her future. She kissed her cheek.

"Go to bed."

"He does respect me. I know that's what is important, and so does he."

"That's good, now let me get on."

"Why don't you want me to marry him?"

"Your father gave his blessing for him to call on you, didn't he? Isn't that enough?"

"But what do you say? I want to know why you are against it."

"Ignore me," she said. "It no longer concerns me. I'm going to Jerez, so do as you please."

"Jerez? Jerez de la Frontera? Spain? Why? You can't leave here and go to Spain!"

"I've told Joseph. Mariquita wants to come with me, but I plan to lose her in the hills along the way. Nacho, I'm certain, will want to stay in Barcelona or Madrid. Tony plans to go to America. Matty will stay with Joseph in London, he won't leave Mary."

"What about Frank? You can't leave him behind with Joseph and Matty."

"Frank will come, but he will not survive the journey. Don't pull that face. You know how ill he is, don't you?"

Tessa breathed in sharply.

"Sandes won't want to leave England."

"You can stay in the house until it is sold. And then you will be married and have a house with Sandes and no more worries."

"Please don't say it like that."

"You will all receive a share of the house. That's all there is left, I'm afraid, and it must be sold and divided up to pay what needs to be paid."

"Was Papa really bankrupt and we have no money?"

"Your father made sure we were taken care of. We are not completely destitute, but the house, well, Joseph may live in the house, and all of you if you wish, I suppose, but for me, I want to go where I have always been happiest."

"Doesn't it bother you what happens to us?"

"You have a lot to learn. I have spent years thinking if I could drive Mariquita away, the rest of you would follow, but you all clung like ivy to stone. When Carmen ran away, I thought, 'Hallelujah! Now they will see that there's a world out there and they will flee,' but you all stuck closer than bees to a honey pot. I don't want to be a honey pot any longer! I don't want to be a wife or a mother. I want to do things for me! I want to live a little before it's too late. Remember, love for a man isn't everything."

TESSA DIDN'T RECOGNISE this woman she thought she'd always known.

"Didn't you love us?" she asked. "Didn't you really love Papa?"

Mrs. Garcia threw up her arms. "That is the point! I loved him more than I loved myself! More than anything else!"

Tessa looked down at the shards of glass on the floor, at the stains on the wall, and she smelt the dried perfume on her skin.

Chapter Twenty-Nine

T HE NOISE IN the tearoom swelled. The efficient waitresses, with their black dresses, white aprons and caps, knew exactly where to be and when. They brought tea and coffee, sandwiches, toast and cakes, all of which were served with a well-practised smile.

Tessa and Sandes sat by the window in silence. In her black dress, Tessa looked like an off-duty waitress herself, and Sandes felt out of place on a weekday afternoon. Fleetingly, he wondered how many Garcia men would die before the younger Garcia women bore sons to replace them.

"My mother sends her condolences," he said.

He wished they had remained in Hyde Park so he could have talked of the horses riding by, of people passing, of the ducks, plane trees, of anything but the death of her unfortunate father.

"Papa liked you," she said as if reading his mind.

"Should I ask the waitress to bring more hot water?"

Tea splashed into her saucer as Tessa lifted her cup.

"Let's go to the National Gallery. That lifted your spirits last time…" His voice trailed away.

"I usually go to Harrods when I'm feeling down."

"Of course. Something pretty."

"I like to smell the perfumes."

"Let's go then." He looked around, trying to catch the waitress's eye. To his annoyance, they were all suddenly inattentive.

"They think we don't need anything, but you are kind."

"That's because I love you."

"I know."

"Why don't you give me one of your beautiful smiles? Show me a little kindness too?"

He was teasing, she'd know that, but it seemed she just couldn't engage. He should have known that too, as he should have known she found comfort in perfume.

"My smiles are all on holiday," she said.

"What do you mean? Holiday?"

A tear ran down her cheek. He fumbled for his handkerchief and, embarrassed, held it out to her.

"I'm sorry," she said, taking it.

"Please, you've nothing to apologise for. I am clumsy."

"I didn't sleep last night."

"You're not yourself."

She laughed. "Who am I then?"

He tried to laugh as well.

"You're lovely."

"I can't do this."

"I know. As soon as one of those blasted waitresses—"

"No, I mean. I haven't finished."

"I didn't say, did I? I want to thank you for not insisting on going to Spain with your mother."

"I'd never insist."

"I know. But thank you for not even going for a holiday. I would have understood, but thank you, anyway. Ah! Here she comes."

"I don't want to marry you."

"Don't worry, I've thought of that." He twisted to face the approaching waitress. "We'll wait. Next spring will be fine."

"I'm not suitable, and I don't want...I mean, I'm not what you want. I'm sorry, but I can't..."

"Of course I want you, my dearest. I love you. You're distraught, that's all, and imagining all sorts. Your father has recently died. It's understandable that you don't know what you want right now. We can't talk about this when you're in mourning. I don't expect you to." He turned to the waitress. "Yes. The bill, please."

The waitress moved away, glancing over her shoulder.

AWARE OF THE tears staining her cheeks, Tessa waited until she was sure she could stop more from pouring forth before she spoke.

"You'll be much happier with someone like Elizabeth Browne."

He was looking across the room after the waitress, his handsome face raised, and she didn't think he'd heard. He would make a good husband. He was a conservative man who would be careful and polite and play with their children on Sunday afternoons.

"I don't know what's wrong with me," she said.

He threw some coins on the tablecloth and prised her to her feet.

"Elizabeth loves you still, no matter what you may think."

"Let's go."

They were moving through the tables. People were watching. Sandes' eyes were fixed on the street beyond the door.

"It's not enough," Tessa said. "There has to be more than love for a lifetime together." They reached the door. "I don't want to lose my nerve."

"Lose your nerve?" he hissed as he took her coat from the rack and held it out.

She put her arms in the sleeves, and he pulled the coat up over her shoulders, holding her close for a second. She felt his hot breath on her neck. Then he was pulling on his own coat.

"Don't make a scene," he whispered. Swooping up his hat and, ushering her before him, he swept her out of the door.

Once on the pavement, she took his hand.

"I want you to be happy," she said.

"Marry me then."

He glanced about them at people walking past.

"I've always had doubts, but now I know why."

Taking her arm, he led her across the street. "Let's drop the conversation. You can't think clearly right now."

"Sandes, stop. I'm right about this. I know I'm right."

He suddenly jerked to a halt, and she swung into him, stepping on his foot.

"What happened to that second chance?" he said, no longer seeming to care about the curious passers-by.

"There are so many might-have-beens." Tears poured down her cheeks again. "I don't want to choose the wrong one."

"I gave *you* a second chance."

"I'm grateful. I am. I love you. I do."

"If you love me, marry me and stop this nonsense."

They began walking again, but quickly this time.

"I've never wanted children, and I don't want to turn out like my mother," she tried to explain.

"Oh, for goodness' sake, you're nothing like your mother."

"Stop. Please stop! We can't talk at this pace, stop!" He halted at the sound of her voice. She took his arm. "Come over here."

She led him to a shop window displaying handbags and leather goods, and he stared at the suitcases, refusing to look at her.

She sighed. "Did you notice how the waitress ignored me?"

"What has that to do with anything?"

"She asked you what we wanted. She checked with you that everything was to our satisfaction. She gave you the bill."

"I asked for it!"

"It always goes to the man."

"What are you saying? Do you want her to give it to you next time? Fine. But you're being ridiculous. A gentleman always pays. Don't you want me to be a gentleman now?"

"I don't want to be invisible."

"You'll be my wife. What can be more visible than that?"

"You don't understand."

"What is there to understand? You'll be Mrs. Sandes and you'll tell people what to do. They'll have to listen to you."

"I want to be Teresa Garcia."

"You are right, I don't understand."

"You don't see how I'll change."

"I want to take care of you, Tessa. You know I love you. Please don't do this. Please stop talking like this."

Tears glistened in his eyes.

TESSA HEARD THE click of his lighter as she left him looking at suitcases in a shop window. She walked swiftly, without looking back. She couldn't look back because if she did, she would see that he had already pulled on the cigarette and that his hollowed cheeks deadened his pink-rimmed eyes. She knew that he would smoke the entire packet, and his insides would be rough and grey and ashen, but she kept on walking. If she turned and saw his erect shoulders and his dark, shining head and smoke billowing out of his mouth, her feet would noisily stampede over the flagstones and she would push her hands into the pockets of his heavy overcoat and feel his scent engulf her, and she would never come up for air again.

Chapter Thirty

TESSA WALKED THROUGH the silent dining room, across the hallway and back again. She didn't pause once to smell the blooms that were past their best. Subconsciously, she heard the difference between the tap of her heels on the wood and her muffled steps over the rugs as she caught a glimpse of her figure moving in the polished surfaces and brass inlay handles of the sideboards.

For a moment, she paused at the foot of the staircase and glanced at the locked front door. It was too late for visitors. Too late for Joseph to check that she was all right. Too late for Mama, Mariquita, Nacho and Frank to change their minds and return. Too late to be downstairs in the empty Garcia house, alone.

Slowly, she mounted the stairs as the last glow of evening sun crept through the downstairs windows and stepped deliberately on the stair that had creaked since she was a child.

Her mother's bedroom was no longer forbidden. The bed covers had been sent in one of the trunks to Spain and the bed looked vast and eerie without them. She slumped on the stool at the dressing table that she had revered all her life. There was nothing there now but a mirror reflecting her face.

That night, she slept in her sister's bed with the sheets pulled up high over her chin. As the first birds began to sing, the sound of footsteps woke her. She lay in bed, waiting for perhaps Abigail to appear, but no-one came. No further sound. She drifted back towards the vividness of early morning dreams, but sensing someone's presence, she opened her eyes. Close to the bedside stood her father.

"It's all right," he said. "I'm watching over you. All will be well."

She blinked, and when she reopened her eyes, her father had gone.

Still in her nightgown, she crossed the landing and peered over the bannisters. It was still too early for the sound of the cook and her pans, or Abigail with her cutlery. This time, Tessa stepped over the creaking stair and paused in the hall for a moment before heading along the corridor, to stand outside her father's study. Skirting his desk, she sat in his chair, curling her feet under her and listened to the quiet of the house. The clock on the mantelpiece had not been wound and had ceased to tick. The portrait of her grandfather had left behind a dark rectangle on the wall. The shelves stood empty of their papers and files, but it was reassuring to still smell leather and a faded sweetness. She hung on to the sense of her father with these smells, and she drew them in. A tap at the door broke her reminiscences.

"Hello?"

Abigail entered.

"I wondered if I'd find you in here," she said. "I've brought the post and *The Times*, Miss. Thought you might want a look before anyone else comes down."

One man she knew well dominated the front page.

"*François Coty is the one perfumier to make his fame from his instinct,*" she read. "*He is not like his predecessors. He comes from nowhere. He does not try to please but goes his own way. He makes his own mistakes, but most notably, his successes. He follows what he likes. He follows above all, the instinct of a killer.*"

Tessa felt she was flying towards the sun. The world opened wide and bright. Maybe her father's words would come true; it would indeed be all right.

Taking the cover from the typewriter, she found a sheet of paper still in the carriage, and began to type. It was only when the letter was finished and folded into an envelope that she headed back upstairs to dress.

Later, Abigail heard her mistress run down the stairs, and she sighed at the bang of the front door.

"That's one less for luncheon," she muttered.

Every day from then on, Tessa sat on the bottom stair, awaiting the post, as she had as a child. First to fall into the cage was her mother's letter, speaking of her arrival in Jerez de la Frontera. She wrote of how she was welcomed back with long meals on the shaded terrace and invitations to tea with all the widows of the region. She did not mention Mariquita, Nacho or Frank.

A few days later, she received a card from Barcelona where Nacho wrote he was going to stay. He did not mention his mother or Mariquita or Frank, only that he had never seen such a city.

Later still, Mariquita's letter arrived. She was staying in a monastery near San Sebastian and told of how the monks had been so grateful to her for the reorganisation of their laundry, so much so that they insisted she visit the neighbouring monasteries and do likewise. They had even furnished her with supplies and her own donkey. She wrote in a way that Tessa had never seen before from Mariquita. There were open spaces in her phrases. There was pride. Above all, she was astonished to witness that her sister did not once mention their mother, Nacho or Frank.

Tessa never received a letter or a card from Frank because on the group's arrival in Spain, Frank had taken his final breath of the gas he'd first breathed in Ypres. Neither she nor any other member of the family ever heard from Tony again, except to find out that he now declared himself an American.

She read out these letters to her father and Alfonso as she sat by their side in the cemetery, knowing that she should be happy for her mother and siblings, that they had found where they belonged, but she was desperate to hear reassurance that she would do the same.

COUPLES AND FAMILIES populated London's pavements and parks. Sandes and Elizabeth Browne dominated the theatres and cricket functions. Tessa remained alone in the house because Joseph and Matty were busy dragging Mr. Jackson towards the justice they felt he deserved. There was much to cling to, and it was only when the Garcia house was sold that she felt completely adrift.

That night, after the sale, she sat at the bottom of the stairs with her hands over her ears and screamed to an empty house.

The next morning, she couldn't keep still, and whirled around the rooms while a voice sang out from the gramophone. Doors banged. Taps released gushing water. Stairs creaked, until, finally, crying could be heard through the door of Mr. Garcia's study.

MRS. GARCIA WAS at last free to stand on mountaintops and on the crests of waterfalls. In Jerez de la Frontera, she, Ann Loughlin once more, opened her mouth and sang to the world with her deep, resounding voice. It bounced off the spray as water poured from under her feet and rushed with music to the deep pools below. Her songs reached across the Mediterranean to Morocco and seeped into the vast reaches of sand. The mountains batted her arias between them until she tossed her voice skywards where it spread through the clouds, flying like a migrating swallow over the Southern Hemisphere.

MARIQUITA, ON THE other hand, wouldn't have recognised joy if it had flown directly in her face. but others recognised it in her demeanour.

Whilst her mother sang of happiness, Mariquita quietly administered peace. Her ability to appear impervious to indifference, ridicule and hatred remained behind in the monasteries she visited, and the monks began to see that her meddling reorganisation was, in fact, a selfless act to provide them with time. With the order she created, when there was no system of order, the monks were freed to concentrate on the godly acts they had been called on to perform. She treated them like a mother who loves all her children equally and forgot about the pastel-coloured statue of the Virgin Mary in a church in London.

Mariquita found that over the months, she was invited back time after time to the monasteries she had first visited on her arrival in Spain. As the years turned to decades, she became a legend, and young monks were told of the large, hairy woman who rode over the hills on a donkey, delivering cleanliness, tranquillity and time with the toughness of an Amazonian, and whom they simply called 'Mama'.

WHILE CARMEN WAS never heard of again by her family, she was indeed alive, well and loving. Carmen adored the many children she bore with the same tactile love she showed Pierre. She remained a child doing adult things, finding that she continued to look whichever priest she met in the eye during her confession or when he ate at her table.

EVENTUALLY, AS CORRESPONDENCE dwindled, a letter addressed to Mademoiselle Garcia arrived.

Abigail wondered who the letter was from but didn't dare ask. The cook announced that the young mistress should have left with the rest of the family.

A FEW DAYS later, a train carried Tessa from London to the White Cliffs of Dover. There, in a fine mist of rain, the cliffs disappeared as she headed for France on a passenger liner. On arrival, she dabbed the perfume Emeraude onto her wrists and behind her ears in preparation for an interview with the great Monsieur François Coty. Finally, she would meet the great perfumier.

Chapter Thirty-One

A<small>S ARRANGED, A</small> car and driver met her at the port, and they headed in the direction of Paris. Watching poplar trees strobe past, she didn't think it strange at first when the Rolls Royce veered through a wide gate and into a field.

Intrigued at the sight of an aeroplane and the chauffeur beckoning her to follow, Tessa stepped out of the car. Her heels sank immediately into the soft ground, and she held on to her hat as a fresh wind blew across the fields from the south. The small aeroplane stood barely a hundred yards away, and as she approached it, her legs began to tremble.

A smartly suited man extended a well-manicured hand, and his sapphire ring glinted in the sunlight.

"Welcome to France, Mademoiselle Garcia."

With effort, she kept her voice steady. "How do you do, Monsieur Coty? I didn't expect to meet you here, sir. I thought it would be in Paris."

He gestured to the open door in the side of the plane. "Are you ready?"

Tessa realised that the interview for which she'd prepared for so long was to take place inside the aeroplane and not where she'd dreamed, in the Château Longchamp or even at Coty's Perfume City.

The chauffeur retreated, and she had to force herself to remain and not follow him back to the car. Coty gestured again to the opening.

"I have never been in an aircraft before," she said.

"Are you willing to change that today?"

It was the last thing she wanted. She'd not been able to look at the sky or hear an engine sound without thinking about Alfonso and how the plane had shrieked to the ground. But she held a Coty-embossed letter in her bag. Her father had assured her all would be well. She had to do this. It was only the same as a car, if she didn't look at the wings. Even so, her legs buckled, she felt sick and she had to battle to keep walking. Glancing at the blue sky and, with a shaking hand, she grasped the side of the plane and forced herself inside.

She could sit there and answer his questions; it was no different to a room. A half hour, an hour at most, and she'd be back in the car, heading to the port and England.

Gripping the seat, she watched Coty sit and look out of the window, and she waited for him to ask his first question. While still waiting, the door slammed closed and Coty fell into shadow. When the engines erupted, she clutched the seat tight. Her heart pounded, and wide-eyed, she watched the grass outside slide past.

"I thought we'd remain on the ground."

"There is no point in remaining on the ground when we're in an aeroplane, Miss Garcia."

Biting her lip, she stared at the field and hedges blurring as the aeroplane's speed increased.

The engines changed pitch, the nose turned upwards, and they left the field behind. There was no getting out now. This wasn't all right. This wasn't what her father had promised. She saw Alfonso's plane, saw the flames, smelt burning, cowed at the sound of shrieking. To avoid showing her complete fear, she looked at the clouds. Her mind filled with the knowledge of the space between them and the hard earth, and she gripped the seat tighter. What could she do?

Sensing Coty's eyes on her, she tried to block out the fact she was sitting in a plane. All the moisture in her mouth evaporated. She swallowed. She needed water. She must be delirious. She couldn't think straight. Gone were the early mornings spent extracting blooms from her mother's displays. Gone were the hours spent pressing petals in the sink in the little bathroom in the Garcia household. Gone were the precious times devoted to being her father's diligent assistant. She sat in dread, empty-hearted, empty-headed and afraid.

"Jacques!" Coty shouted. "Cut the engines!"

From far, far away, came a response.

"And the usual?"

Coty kept his gaze on her face. "That goes without saying."

She swallowed again, trying to find enough moisture there to enable speech. How could it get any worse? Perhaps she could scrape moisture from her clammy skin. She licked her lips.

"I don't know much about engines, Monsieur Coty," she said, "but won't that mean that we have no power?"

"Correct."

She licked her lips again.

"Won't having no power mean that the plane will fall?"

"You know more about engines than you think," he said. "It is what is called a nosedive."

They listened to the silence. She saw a plane with its tail of fire and heard a long, terrified scream. Tears simmered in her eyes.

"Will we not... Will that mean...that... We will..."

"Crash?"

The wind rushed outside. The plane began to shudder. He glanced at her hands, clutching the seat.

"Do you trust the pilot?" he asked.

"I haven't got much choice."

"Do you trust that I would only choose the best pilot?"

"I know you love aeroplanes. You won't want to crash it."

"What is it that you can offer me, Miss Garcia? I offer you the best pilot to save your life. What can you offer me?"

He shouted. The engines roared. She wanted to scream.

"I am a practising Catholic," she said. "I have faith."

"Admirable, but not a prerequisite, and I doubt it will stop a plane crashing."

"It means I am not afraid to die."

The trail of falling blasted louder.

"Nor are many atheists."

She could barely hear the words for the searing screech of the engine.

"I gave up a safe, secure future to work for you."

"Giving up a safe, secure future is easy."

She could barely hear her own words over the pounding of air.

"It's not easy for females," she said. "My father, my brother…"

Her words trembled, and she stuttered to a halt. These weren't the answers she'd planned on using, nor were they the questions she'd expected him to ask.

"I never give up," she said.

He turned his head to the window and she squeezed back the tears.

"I have the killer instinct," she blurted. "I gave up love to work for you."

There was nothing more to say. What else could she do? They were falling, and any moment they would crash into the ground, and he didn't care that he'd die or she'd die or that the pilot would die. The plane screamed. She wasn't ready to give in. Her father had said it would be all right, and she believed he had really stood at her bedside. She released her hold on the seat. Leaning forwards, desperate to grab the side of the plane, she stood, splaying her arms, balancing, swaying, readying to fall on her knees.

"I want to fly," she said. "You read my letter, you responded. I am ready to fly."

Holding her stance, she stared at him. He didn't blink, and then, just when she anticipated the pain of the crash, Coty clicked his fingers, and as her stomach lurched, a sense of disbelief flowered as the engine reignited.

"What perfume do you wear?" he asked as she sat down.

Her voice shook. "Today, I'm wearing—"

Coty held up one hand to silence her. He undid his safety belt and crouched on the floor at her feet. She remained still while he placed his hands on the arms on either side. His hair brushed gently across her right cheek as he breathed in. She held her breath, listening to the drone of the engine and feeling his breath on her skin, and she smelt sandalwood on his.

His face was inches from her own, and they stared in silence at each other, Coty, with one eye fixed, the other sparkling. And then, just as suddenly, he pushed himself to his feet.

"You may take us down, Jacques," he shouted.

The muffled voice of the pilot again. "To Suresnes, sir?"

"Suresnes. If instinct tells me right, Miss Garcia, it is time to meet your new family."

Family. She hadn't expected to hear that word ever again.

Staring out of the window at field upon field of brightly coloured flowers stretching into the distance, she savoured the word. Thoughts of death vanished, and in their place, the thrill of new beginnings. It would be all right. The plane tilted, and the windows filled with reds, blues, whites and yellows. Below them, sweeps of scent beckoned. Suresnes, Coty's Perfume City, and a new family promised a new home. They tilted again, and a shadow followed them across the meadows.

The End

About the Author

Ruth Estevez lives in Manchester where she works as project coordinator for The Portico Sadie Massey Awards for Young Readers and Writers, based at The Portico Library.

Ruth has previously worked as a scriptwriter on the children's TV series *Bob the Builder* and worked in theatre and TV from Opera North, Harrogate Theatre-in-Education Company, Pitlochry Festival Theatre to *Emmerdale*. She has also taught scriptwriting on the Contemporary BA Film and Television Course at Manchester Metropolitan University.

When not writing or project coordinating, Ruth is either dancing or indulging in her latest passion, long-distance walking.

You can contact Ruth on...

Instagram: @ruthestevezwriter
Twitter: @RuthEstevez2
Facebook:- @RuthEstevezM
Website: www.artgoesglobal.wordpress.com

By the Author

Erosion

Jiddy Vardy

Jiddy Vardy – High Tide

Jiddy Vardy 3 – coming 2022

The Monster Belt

Meeting Coty (2nd Edition)

Beaten Track Publishing

For more titles from Beaten Track Publishing,
please visit our website:

https://www.beatentrackpublishing.com

Thanks for reading!

Ingram Content Group UK Ltd.
Milton Keynes UK
UKHW042210110723
424969UK00005B/113

9 781786 455321